Nykur

***

G D Iversen

For my Dad

Chapter 1

The crashing noise of falling objects broke the silence of the old farmhouse and the quiet musings of Hugh in his room. He sprung from his bed and crossed the landing, taking the stairs two at a time in his haste.

"Dylan?" he called as he ran, his bare feet slapping against the cracked tile floor with every step. The living room was unlit, so he passed without hesitation. Only the faint noise of the television came from within. From the kitchen came the cries of his younger brother. He threw open the door to find him stood by the sink. The front of his clothes appeared wet and the surrounding floor was scattered with pans and pieces of Dylan's favourite train mug. The boy's crying persisted. Hugh dropped to his level and took his shoulders in his hands.

"Dylan? Are you hurt?" he asked. His brother shook his head and began to sniff as his tears subsided.

"I tried to get a drink from the tap but I knocked the pots on the floor and now my cup is broken," he said, and his statement of the fact brought on a fresh wave of crying.

"It's ok, it's ok. I can clear this up."

"But Hugh, I'm hungry." He fixed Hugh with wide eyes.

"Has mum not got up yet?" Dylan shook his head again. Hugh straightened and tried to summon some energy. He could not deny the ache of hunger deep in his own stomach; they both needed a meal.

He found a damp tea towel left on top of a stack of old letters on the counter and dropped it on the mess of shattered ceramic to soak up the water. With some disgust he gathered the fallen, dirty pans, and reset them in their stack next to the sink. He then finished clearing away the broken cup. Much to Dylan's dismay, he insisted that it could not be repaired.

There was nothing new in the cupboards; only dusty sauces,

herbs and some tinned fruit graced the shelves. The fridge proved no better, harbouring assorted fruit juice and some vegetables that pooled in their own mould. Dylan sat waiting at the table, tracing his finger on the cover. The bread bin housed many empty cellophane wraps, but in one Hugh uncovered an end piece of bread and without too close an inspection put it in the toaster. He warmed some beans and put them on the toast for Dylan with a cup of squash. He sat watching his brother eat, his hunger clear by the lack of complaint or any pause to speak. When his own stomach growled, he pushed his chair to cover the noise and crossed his arms tighter.

"Where's Mum?" Hugh asked his brother as he cleared the plate.

"She's in the living room," Dylan replied. Hugh's mouth tightened into a grim line. "My clothes are still wet."

He took his little brother upstairs and helped him remove the wet clothes, but finding no clean pyjamas in the drawers, persuaded him he would be warm enough to go without. He tried to settle his brother in bed, but in his distraction found it difficult.

"I want you to stay in bed. It's time to sleep," he said.

"Are you going to get mum up?"

"Yes, so don't come downstairs. See you in the morning, go to sleep."

Dylan watched his big brother cross through his messy bedroom and retreat through the door. The house was quiet again.

Hugh navigated the exposed floorboards of the landing piled with clutter in every corner and edge as he returned downstairs. This time he made a beeline for the living room. The glare from a sports programa was all that lit the otherwise dark and silent space. Its sole inhabitant was in the furthest corner, positioned within an old armchair dull with wear and stains. A woman in deep repose, his mother, was half sprawled and slumped to the side. The light from the television screen touched upon one pallid cheek. She appeared to be at rest, but Hugh knew better.

His entrance had still yet elicited no response from the figure in the chair, so with one hand he felt for the light switch, flicking it on.

"Mum wake up," he said, and watched as the eye he could now see closed tighter against the flood of light. "You need to get some food, there's nothing in the house."

He waited for a reply, but only the sound of the television continued. Spotting the remote on the floor he turned it off, placing it on what small space of coffee table he could see between its cover of old magazines and assorted paper and food wrappers.

"Wake up!" he shouted. His chest rose and fell with every breath. He was looking for any sign from his mother that she would get up, make some food, do anything. Her eyes had relaxed, but still shut out the world.

Outside, the cool evening breeze pushed its way through the darkening canopy of leaves that shaded the sparse woodland path below. The gentle collective rustle of leaves did not mute the sound of breaking twigs and crushed undergrowth beneath the worn, leather boots of the old man, who took just one more step before dropping to a crouch position.

"Stay there, Sanna." he breathed, craning for a better look between the last line of trees in front of them. The man took in heavy breaths as he surveyed the land ahead. A well-aged, stone farmhouse occupied the far end of the space before him. It was overgrown grassland, dotted with detritus and a rusted play frame. Unkempt ivy crept over the windows of the house, of which a few lit windows brightened an otherwise grey vista, and in parts the exterior stone crumbled.

Behind him came the sound of hooves imprinting in the ground. Sanna reached his shoulder and exhaled warm breath against the back of his neck.

"No closer. They might see us."

He made a careful scan of the area around the house, taking an interest in what appeared to be outbuildings and a shed of some description. Beyond them, a driveway merged its edges with the land. There was a hefty nudge at his back. He turned and placed a weathered, four-fingered hand against the dark grey of her velvet muzzle. The horse dipped her white head and let his scarred hand run up the length of it to meet her dark forelock before she raised it again sharply and fixed him with molten eyes.

"I know, I know. Just one moment."

He looked again at the house and saw movement by what must be the back door. A teenage boy huddled in an oversized sweatshirt was struggling with a rubbish sack. He put it in a dustbin and paused for a moment, inhaling the night air. His mouth fixed in a grim line as he returned inside.

"I think we might have found somewhere to stay."

Chapter 2

With some reluctance, Hugh peeked around the bedroom door of his Mother who was curled foetus like in imitation of sleep. He opened his mouth to speak and go through the standard procedures of a school morning, but on seeing her static form fully clothed under the bedsheets, he decided otherwise. He went to his brother's room.

"Are you awake?" he asked, registering the faint flicker of an eyelid and the twitch of Dylan's mouth. With no reply, he gathered up the dirty clothes that lay about the floor around the bed. He knew from yesterday that his brother was out of clean clothes.

"You need to get up. I'm going to school today."

"I don't feel well," Dylan said. Hugh studied him, trying to detect any trace of a lie. He knew of his dislike of Monday mornings.

"What's wrong?"

"Headache and my throat hurts." Dylan replied, forcing a weak cough to back this up. Hugh closed the distance between them, placing a hand across his forehead to test the temperature. He noticed it was warm, warmer than usual he wasn't sure, but another feeble cough was enough for him to give in.

"Get some sleep. I'll bring up some medicine before I leave."

After a quick breakfast, he darted back upstairs to give Dylan a cup of water and Calpol, trusting him to take it. It was all he had time for.

Outside, a gust of unseasonable wind put his carefully tousled hair out of place the moment he stepped onto the drive. He glanced up at the sky, squinting at the bright summer sun before throwing his pack onto his shoulder and setting off for the bus stop, head down, shoulders hunched. His morning commute to the bus stop was often his favourite part of the day, being the only peaceful one. It gave him the space and quiet for thinking, musing over whatever took his fancy. He never felt under any pressure to rush or walk fast. The straight road of the village allowed a clear view of the bus stop from almost the bottom of his drive. If the bus arrived before he did, he still wouldn't break into a run. He was beyond caring in the way that most people would. He could be late without consequence, not attend without rebuttal. Others might take notice and intervene after a time, maybe then his mother would act on his account, but he attended by his own choice, he enjoyed the company and the change of setting.

A large stone stood in the path of his foot. He kicked it as he reached the bus stop, watching as it skimmed past the red trainers of his friend Kain.

"Morning Hugh," he said with a smile, slapping him across the shoulder with forceful good humour.

"How's it going?" Hugh replied with a dip of his head. "Where's Ben?"

"Still asleep probably knowing him."

The bus appeared and with it, the sight of Ben dashing from out of a side street and running towards them. Kain broke into a laugh.

"Here he is. Come on Ben, you can run quicker than that."

Ben reached them just as the bus pulled up. He was too busy catching his breath to speak. The double doors drew apart and Kain moved between the two younger girls with them to get first in line. The three of them took seats at the back of the bus, Kain occupying two as he sat slouched with his legs spread.

"Busy weekend then?" Kain asked him.

"Not really, just spent it at home with Dylan. I was meant to see Liana, but I slept through most of Sunday in the end."

"Has she been messaging you a lot?"

"Now and then." He replied. Kain stared into his eyes for a few seconds, his dark eyebrows drawn together. Through the window, Hugh watched the trees and hedgerows fly past in an unfocused blur.

"I know you don't do parties but you should've come to Gaz's Saturday, it was lit."

"It was," Ben said, rooting around in his rucksack for food. "It was well worth the grief from my mum when I got back, put it that way."

"Yeah well I would've but I had to stay with Dylan." Kain didn't reply, he was too busy scrolling through his music collection.

"Hugh, you want to come to mine after school? I got some new FIFA cards."

"I can't, Dylan's ill; maybe tomorrow."

"I'll be there," Kain said. "Only a few more days boys, then we won't have to bother with school for the summer."

Hugh sat back and rested his head against the seat. Now that he'd dealt with the ritual questions, he could relax.

The school day passed with no major event, and when the bell rang, Hugh made a solitary journey home. Dylan was in the living room still in his pyjamas and dancing to garish music from one of his favourite cartoons. When he saw Hugh in the doorway, he froze as if playing musical statues before skulking to the sofa to sit.

"What are you doing? You're supposed to be ill." Hugh said, looking over the empty cups, crisp packets and DVD cases that lay in evidence of the day's activity.

"I am ill, but I was feeling a little better," Dylan said in a small voice, his hands twisting around each other. Hugh exhaled in exasperation.

"I'm not stupid, you know," he told him, gathering up the rubbish to put in the bin. Dylan followed him to the kitchen. "Has mum been up today?"

"Not for long. I tried to wake her up when the phone was ringing but she didn't want to."

Hugh put a load in the washing machine, sticking it on high. He expected his mother to be up within the next couple of hours. All he wanted to do after a day at school was kick off his shoes and relax, but Dylan had other ideas. He fetched his old wellies and pulled them on.

"Let's play outside. Come on, we can go in the woods."

"You're in pyjamas," he said.

"I don't mind. Please!" Hugh was less than enthusiastic about the prospect, but he knew from experience that his younger brother was a lot easier to settle when he'd had the chance to run off some energy.

"Ok then. But not for too long." This was all the encouragement Dylan needed to see him racing out the door, leaving Hugh to take a last sip of water before following him into the sprawling land that backed onto the farmhouse. He faced a sea of green from what remained of the small patio on which he stood. The paving was in dire need of re-levelling and long shoots of dandelions were pushing through the gaps. The area of land that had once passed for a decent garden had since reverted to a wild state. Grass of all varieties had grown without restriction and reclaimed any landscaping efforts that once were. There was some sparse play equipment, once loved, a wooden frame that Hugh himself had once enjoyed. They were now hidden amongst the jungle of growth, finding them being half of the fun.

"Why don't we play in the garden?" Hugh called. "We don't

need to go into the woods."

Dylan was already close to the trees that lined the border of the land they called home. They formed a tall, dark sentry that contrasted with the blue sky overhead.

"I want to," Dylan replied. "It'll be cooler in there under the trees, won't it Hugh?"

"Should be," he said, catching up with his brother at a jog. Dylan's happy face turned up to his, flushed from the heat of the day.

They met with the small space between the trees where bare dirt marked a crude path leading into the woodland. Dylan skipped ahead, stopping at intervals to check the undergrowth for any interesting finds. Hugh was distracted by his phone until he noticed his brother taking an interest in a partially concealed side path that passed among the ferns and through the boughs to their right.

"Does this go to the river Hugh?" he asked.

"If I remember right, I don't want to be out here for too long though."

Without further conversation, Dylan bolted down the path. Hugh put away his phone and kept his brother in sight as he followed what he could see of the track. It curved to the left, a break in the thick mass of trees revealing a clearing. Beech trees stood at its edge, their highest branches not quite meeting overhead, letting the sunlight brighten the dirt in the open space. At its other end was the river, cutting its route through the woods like a vein. The ground sloped down to the bank, meeting the water where it flowed wide and shallow over a rocky bed, with thick woodland encroaching on the opposite bank.

Hugh had been here before. In a time when going to the woods would elicit as much excitement as Dylan now enjoyed. His dad had brought him here when Hugh could rely on him, before it had ever entered his mind that things could change. Dylan rushed to the river's edge and looked into the water. Hugh moved to join him but caught sight of what looked like the remains of a fire, a small patch of ash that marred the blackened ground.

"Is there fish in here?" Dylan called. Hugh scuffed the ashes into the ground with the toe of his trainers. "Hugh?"

"I guess, maybe some," he said. Dylan was content for a few minutes throwing sticks and stones into the flowing water.

"If we throw enough in, we could stop the water!" Dylan shouted.

"Like a dam, right?"

"Yeah."

Hugh helped Dylan to find the best sticks with which to build their dam, pausing at a patch of scattered dry logs, an involuntary memory of helping his dad to collect firewood. He turned away, looking for long branches he could drag across the ground. This occupied both of them for a time, but Hugh's unwillingness to get his feet wet proved a limit to their progress. Dylan kept up his attempt with bright optimism, throwing sticks increasingly far to extend his blockade to the far bank, but his aim was not accurate and his mind soon became distracted. It had been thirty minutes and Hugh was reaching the end of his tolerance for kid's play after school.

"We're going back in a minute. It's getting late."

"Ok, but I need to get something first," Dylan said, running towards the nearest trees on a hunt for a wooden sword. Hugh studied the river in front of where he stood. He could see the rocks and the weeds that existed under the water. Further on, the river was dark; smooth where it didn't meet high rocks beneath that mottled the surface. He watched the water pass without a sound until a faint thud made him look up. He saw a white horse stood amongst the trees straight ahead of him. It stepped forward under the eaves of a broad oak, giving each a clear sight of the other. Her white coat shone as if slicked with oil and the length of her mane and tail were dark grey in contrast. She fixed him with a cold, curious stare.

Behind him, Hugh heard the onset of crying from Dylan. He turned to see him emerging from the trees clutching his knees and heaving with large, wet sobs that shook his body. He rushed to his side, seeing that he'd fallen in some nettles. He wasn't able to stop his tears, and with no dock leaves nearby he reassured his brother they would head straight home and come back another day. He held his hand as they made a slow walk back to the path they'd come in from. When Hugh looked back to the river, the horse had gone. The clearing was empty.

Chapter 3

Hugh stopped by Dylan's room and gathered him some clothes from the rough pile of the washing he'd done the previous day. He didn't bother to check on his mother, leaving her bedroom door undisturbed. He was, however, grateful to find that she'd been out last night and fetched some supplies; It made providing breakfast for him and his brother a lot easier. He left home with the promise of returning soon, and that it wouldn't be long until Dylan had him for the summer break.

He'd long missed the first bus, so sat on the ground, fiddling with his laces and thinking about his friends. Light footsteps interrupted his thoughts, and when he looked up, he saw Liana standing almost over him, arms crossed.

"I see you're late too then?" he said, getting to his feet. She shrugged.

"I overslept, couldn't be bothered to rush."

"Really? And what did your mum have to say about that?"

"She wasn't happy obviously. But like I told her, it's practically the holidays; no one's going to care." She looked at him, her blue eyes fixing him intently for a moment whilst he was looking at the floor. "Have you cheered up since the weekend?"

"Yeah sorry about that, I was having a bad day."

"When don't you have one of those Hugh?" she asked him, adjusting her hair.

"Hey," he said, "Me and Kain are planning to go to Ben's after school; you can join us if you want." Liana paused whilst she spent a moment considering the offer.

"Thanks, but I've got stuff to do at home. I would like to see you someday though."

"Another time," he said, one side of his mouth turning up in effect of a smile.

Hugh sat cross-legged on the blue cover of Ben's bed, watching as he retrieved a hidden stash of sweets and opened them to share. He'd spent the entire school day looking forward to this. The PlayStation fired up and Kain took his position with the controller. Ben lay next to Hugh, helping himself to handfuls of food. The room was soon quiet with the sound of FIFA and content chewing.

"Last day of school tomorrow then lads," Kain said. "Going to be a good summer, I reckon." Both Hugh and Ben made noises of agreement.

"I can't wait," Ben said, still chewing.

"You guys got much planned for the summer?" Hugh asked.

"Not really. I'll just be trying to stay out the house." Kain replied.

"I've got to go to Grimsby, we've got family up there." Ben chipped in, sounding glum. Hugh thought it sounded nice to get the chance to go somewhere new. There was a knock at the door. Ben's mum peered in at them.

"You're not eating all that are you?" Ben swallowed what he had been enjoying and slipped both hands under his sizeable thighs. "Dinner will be ready in a minute."

"Ok mum," he replied. The door closed. "She never leaves me alone." He sighed.

Time passed quickly and Hugh declined his invitation for dinner, wanting to get home and check on Dylan. It was a ten-minute walk to his house. Being summer, the early evening was mild and still bright, but the roads were empty. As he turned up onto the hill of his drive and looked up to the old farmhouse that he'd called home for most of his life, he could take no clue as to the activity of its occupants. All the windows were dark squares.

He let himself in and walked almost to the stairs before he found any evidence of life. Dylan rushed to greet him from the living room with outstretched arms, but to his dismay, Dylan wasn't the only voice to meet him.

"Hugh? Is that you?" his mother spoke from the darkened space beyond the door, the curtains still drawn from the previous night.

"Yes."

"Where have you been? You didn't tell me you were going out," she said. Hugh pushed open the door and switched on the light. His mother squinted in her seat.

"How can I tell you things when you're always asleep?"

"Hugh, will you watch your attitude please? If I had known you wouldn't be here, I'd have made sure I was up and watching Dylan."

"You're supposed to be awake and looking after him all the time. That's what parents are supposed to do."

"Stop shouting," she said, and Hugh could tell by the crumpling of her face that tears were imminent. He hated nothing more.

"I should be able to see some friends if I want to," he said, his chest feeling hot and tight. He turned to walk out of the room, stepping around Dylan who had been listening. "I'm going out again if you must know. Don't forget to feed Dylan, by the looks of it you haven't already," he called over his shoulder.

Not having taken off his shoes, all he did as he passed through the kitchen was grab an apple from the counter. He stepped into the garden and already felt better than he did inside the gloomy, cluttered confines of the house. He cut a direct route through the long grass to slip under the shade of the woods. It was much quicker without having to check behind him in concern for his young brother. He held an apple by his side; he was sure horses were meant to like them. He'd find out if he found one.

His quick step broke into a steady jog, a sense of urgency taking hold. He hopped over the tree roots that had freed themselves from the ground and encroached on the path, spotting the side trail just as he was about to pass it. He slowed to a walk, trying to steady his breathing and concentrate on his surroundings. The clearing was quiet, still; he studied it for a moment before stepping into the open space. The river was calm, the water tranquil and emitting only the faintest sound where it hit against the grey protrusions of rock. He stopped less than a metre from the edge, seeing nothing except the trees and the dark spaces in between. The low setting sun cast long shadows on the ground, making the trunks appear black. The last light filtering through the oak's vast spread of leaves like a child's finger painting made with every shade of green.

He turned from the river and wandered to the left, looking for anything out of place. Movement caught his eye. In the treeline closest to him, a pale shape moved through the foliage with slow, heavy steps. Hugh watched as it came closer, not daring to move. The horse didn't seem to have noticed him. It stood among the low tangle of ivy with its head lowered to the ground, its thick mass of mane trailing in the dirt. Its coat was smooth and shiny as though wet. Now that he was so near, he could make out the slight dapples of grey that speckled her shoulder and spread across her rump. She was female.

The creature raised her head and looked straight at him. He found himself met with eyes black as obsidian, which appraised him with a surprising sharpness. Her pink nostrils flared to take in his scent, every muscle taut with tension. They faced each other, each trying to discern the other's intention. He remembered the apple he had brought from the house and held it out in front of him, offering it to the animal that pricked her ears with interest. Feeling encouraged, he approached her slowly, letting his feet ease onto the ground with each step to mute any noise underfoot. He was close enough for her to take the fruit in his outstretched hand. The horse reached her muzzle forward to take in the apple's smell whilst keeping a watchful eye on the boy. He began to relax, but then the horse tossed her head violently skyward and sent him stumbling back beneath the sight of her wild, rolling eyes. The apple fell to the ground with a dull thud and the horse began to calm again, although he could tell she was ready to run.

The horse's gaze once again morphed from cautious to curious, and feeling brave, Hugh reached a shaky hand to the mid-air that stood in between them. She dropped her head to meet it and the feel of her whiskers surprised him, wiry and coarse. He was also shocked by the icy cool of her breath, that she exhaled in deep huffs as she took in his smell. He pulled his hand back to his side, still watching to see her reaction. Her ears pricked to follow his hand and he smiled as he felt the previous tension dispel.

Close to her now, he placed his palm against her wither, feeling her flinch at his touch. Her coat was cool and had a damp, sticking quality to it. It felt unpleasant, like the outer of an empty dead thing rather than the living, breathing body of such a large animal. Deciding she must be cold, he thought he'd fetch a towel to dry her and so backed away to return to the house. She watched him leave like a quiet omen. He stumbled on the rutted ground as he left the clearing behind, the sun's reach diminishing now. Once out of the woodland and in the wilderness of his back garden, he sprinted to the back door.

Inside, Dylan was still up. He had eaten but was not in bed. By the time Hugh had taken care of his brother and cleared enough kitchen space to make an adequate snack to sleep on, the sun had fully set. The horse would probably be gone by now, and so with the prospect of hunting around a dark woods not appealing to him, he opted to kick off his trainers in his room and get some rest.

Chapter 4

Hugh stood amongst the moving crowd of excited teenagers, streaming out of their classrooms to leave school for the holidays. He waited, taking the hits of stray, passing elbows until he had space to move. He crossed the corridor and took the single flight of stairs to the top floor. He was just in time; The first door on his right sprung open and released its occupants. When Liana appeared, he took her arm and pulled her to the side.

"Oh, it's you. What's up?" she asked with a surprised smile, dismissing her friends.

"Come round mine, there's something I want to show you."

"Sure, can I go home and get changed first?"

"Fine," Hugh replied. "Just text me when you're there."

There were too many of her friends around to stay with her. His priority was getting away from the school grounds. At home, he found Dylan dressed and getting creative with his pens. His mother was in bed. He changed out of his uniform and heard his phone go off. Dylan followed him as he raced back down the stairs, wanting to go with him, but Hugh instructed him to stay, reassuring him they would play his choice of board game when he was back.

He met her at the top of the drive where behind the house it opened up to a small concrete space lined with rusting junk and dilapidated outbuildings that stored the shells of equipment long forgotten. She had changed into frayed denim shorts and a pale, bohemian style vest. Her long, honey coloured hair hung free by her shoulders.

He led her through the narrow passage that took them past the back door and into the grassland beyond.

"We're heading out back?" she asked.

"Yeah, to the woods."

"Oh, right," she said, trying to keep up with him. "How's your mum? And your brother, he was so small when I last saw him, he must be grown big now."

"Yeah, he's growing fast." He had no intention of inviting her in to the house. He was concentrating on the route through the grass.'

"So I guess I'll see for myself whatever it is you want to show me."

"Hopefully," he said. "If she's there."

He led her to the clearing, both having to watch where they put their feet. Liana watched as Hugh paced first to one side, then the other. He listened. She watched him go to the river's edge, the toe of his sneaker almost contacting the water as he seemed to study the opposite bank. The thick growth of trees made it hard to get a clear view of any distance. After a minute he turned back to her and sat on the ground. She joined him, trying not to think about getting dirt on her new shorts.

"She's not here," he stated. Liana's brow furrowed.

"Who's not here?"

"There was a white horse here. I saw her the other day when I came with Dylan. Last night she was here again, I touched her."

"That's weird; you don't get wild horses round here. Maybe it's escaped or something. It's got to belong to someone."

"You know about horses?" he asked.

"Yeah, I used to ride."

"Do you know if they like apples?" Liana looked bemused.

"Yes, of course." Hugh was quiet for a moment, pulling at a stray patch of grass by his shoe. He remembered the horse's reaction to the apple he'd offered the previous night. "Maybe it'll show up if we wait a while." Hugh squinted at the bank, the dirt bare and undisturbed.

"I don't think so. I don't think it's coming back. "

They sat in companionable silence for a few minutes, both mulling over the day and waiting to see if anything would join them.

"Have you heard about the party next Friday?" Liana said. "You should come, it'll be good. I know Kain's going."

"Maybe." He shrugged. "If I'm free, then I'll consider it."

"Come on, you never come out to anything. You'd probably enjoy getting out and socialising for once." He looked at her.

"It's not a priority of mine to get flat wasted in the company of strangers."

"I'll be there," she said. He got to his feet, easing the cramp from his legs.

"Remind me nearer the time. I can't promise."

Back at the house, they came through the alleyway and paused by the door. She paused as if waiting for something, and he realised that social norms would expect him to invite her in. He stepped towards the drive, his hands deep in his pockets.

"I'll see you around then," he said. Liana took his cue and left, pulling out her phone as she set out to walk back to her own home.

He met Dylan inside, and after some food he made good on his promise to play board games. He let him stay up for an extra hour then both boys went to bed, although it was another three before Hugh resigned to sleep.

The first week of the holidays passed with the exact monotony expected by Hugh, because really it was the same as any other time the law didn't require him to be out of the house. At least in the initial first days there was some novelty in getting to sleep in and take his time to dress in the morning.

Dylan loved nothing more than having Hugh's company in sitting through the day's entire cartoon showings in their pyjamas, shielded from the ever brightening sun outside by the drawn curtains of the living room. The dimness hid the mess they sat in.

His thoughts rarely touched upon his encounter with the strange horse in the woods. He just assumed she'd left after her absence when he'd waited with Liana, and he'd been spending an increased amount of time thinking about the upcoming party in the quiet moments he had to himself. It surprised him to entertain the idea, but after a week of days that merged into one another, confined within the house or its immediate area, the prospect of going out and spending time with people his own age became more and more tempting. His mother had been at a low ebb of functioning since the break from school. Most days he only saw her in the evenings when she'd take an hour to drink a single cup of tea and form a coherent word let alone function on any practical level. Despite this, she had made a few shopping trips and the house had food, so they had avoided any arguments.

Friday came and Hugh read over and re-read the details Liana had sent him via text. The clock told him it was just past nine which gave him forty minutes to get changed and walk to the house in the estate where it was happening. He held his phone in his right hand, his finger hovering over the reply button. She had messaged him yesterday after he told her he'd come along, but he'd heard nothing from her since. He threw open the doors of his wardrobe, all his regular clothes were in various states of disarray around his room but he was looking for an item of clothing he hadn't worn since his aunt's wedding two years previous. It was on a lone hanger on the far left side of the rail. He picked out the light blue shirt and tried it on. It was tighter than he would prefer but he thought it passable. It was the only thing clean and ironed at any rate. He swapped his joggers for the least worn pair of jeans on his floor and thought he looked suitable as long as nobody paid too close attention.

He crossed the landing to his mother's room, throwing open the door to find her wrapped up with the duvet that had tangled around her legs like an oversized, beige cocoon.

"Mum," he said. "Mum wake up. I'm going out." His mother didn't move from her position, although his voice reached her ears from the rectangle of light at the doorway. Hugh resigned himself to the fact that she wasn't going to get up. He had not the energy or inclination to try to change the fact. He turned and left, leaving the door open to allow a better chance of her hearing Dylan if he needed her.

Downstairs his younger brother was full of questions when he noticed Hugh's change of clothes. He told him he'd be out seeing friends for a bit and put on Dylan's favourite Spy Dogs DVD to keep him entertained. With one last check of his phone he could leave the house, stepping outside into the mild but breezy evening with a fresh wave of excitement. At least he thought it was excitement at first. Within a moment's pause for consideration, the wind had turned biting and the sky seemed turbulent. He thought of the drinking, the girls, the banter and the loud, pulsing music that would beat so loud that it seemed to vibrate through your very blood. His lungs compressed and his heart shifted up a gear. He knew that if he did not set out to the party now, he would not go. If he was honest with himself, he didn't want to; but the door was shut behind him and he wanted less to go back inside. He needed time for himself.

He got moving, and once the house was out of sight behind him and his arms were swinging free at his sides as he passed through the dark, empty streets, he didn't feel half bad. He guessed it was exhilaration that made his heart race and emboldened him, although when he got near to the house and saw the crowd of youths his age and older spilling out of the door and milling around the entrance, it exited down and through his feet, dissipating into the night and taking all his confidence with it.

His phone went off in his hand and the sudden noise made him jump. It was a text from Liana asking if he was still coming. He read it without opening it and then locked his screen, keeping it in his hand. A sudden painful self-awareness struck as a multitude of eyes locked on him. They all looked the same stood in the dim glow from the house's windows. It was a small semi; the garden was a scruff of land and the path was hazardous, but he crossed it without tripping and found himself at the doorway with no other option but to push past the black-clad people who had left only a slip of space for him to gain entry.

He paused, wondering if he should instead perhaps ask them to move, but his voice was still hidden away beyond retrieval. He turned side on and squeezed through the small gap, brushing against someone's shoulder as he did.

"Hey. Watch it." He heard a deep voice say in his right ear and what seemed to be a great cloud of acrid cigarette smoke washed over him, scorching the top of his throat in his next two breaths. He shuffled away, looking around for anyone he knew, but the house was disorienting and full of unfriendly faces. He heard a commotion coming from the large room to his left. He was looking for Liana and to his relief he saw her. She had been gazing in the door's direction as he entered. Her face lit up, and she rushed toward him.

"Hugh, you made it."

"Yeah," he said, not bothering to compete with music someone had turned up too high. "I don't know anyone here." He spoke louder this time, realising she probably hadn't heard him before.

"Don't worry," she replied. "Come with me."

Glittery eyeshadow spread from her eyelid to her brow. Her eyes were bright and blue, dancing with excitement as she jumped up to speak closer to his ear, her propped hand raising her cup out of any danger. She turned towards a raucous group nearby, expecting him to follow. She stopped at a small side table laden with cheap plastic cups and various alcoholic drinks. She poured him a drink without him being able to see what it was. He knew by the smell before it even reached his lips that it would taste foul. On his tongue it tasted like the cool sweetness of cordial, but at the swallow the sweetness was gone and what replaced it was a dragon that protested its consumption hotly. He pursed his lips and vowed to sip no more. In the time since first tasting some wine his mother had left uncorked one night, the taste of alcohol had made no improvement.

He stayed on the outer edge of the group she returned to. The only person he knew apart from Liana was Kain, who stood right in the centre. The colour was high in Kain's cheeks and by the exaggerated movement of his arms and upper body it was obvious that he was already well acquainted with the drink this evening. He had little interest in getting involved in whatever it was they found so amusing. Liana was all smiles. She was talking with girls he'd never seen her with before, but with her bodycon dress and perfectly arranged hair she fit right in, at least on the surface. Having known her since reception, Hugh knew that for a long time she had shunned the lure of makeup and the glossy ads of fashion and celebrity infatuation, dismissing it as facile and shallow. She had always been fresh faced and confident in her bare skin and inquisitive mind. She had remained loyal with girls who, like her, preferred to spend their break time playing sport or discussing books over gossip or incessant boy chasing. He imagined them being kicked to the curb in favour of this new crowd. She sipped on her drink every few seconds.

Kain had quietened down and stepped away from the centre of attention now, leaving another lad to take a turn. He kept glancing towards Liana, and after a minute his gaze fell upon Hugh. They appraised each other through the crowd, the music still thudding on, mixing with the thrum of conversation and sending out the pulse of a powerful bass that made focus difficult. He downed the rest of his drink, tossing the cup to the floor before approaching him.

"I wasn't expecting to see you here."

"Liana invited me." Hugh replied. Kain shot another glance to Liana who smiled and tucked her free arm across her stomach. His eyes darted back to Hugh.

"Enjoying it?"

"Not really."

Kain made a dismissive sound and reached for one of his pockets. He pulled out a packet of cigarettes but stopped before opening it, instead running his fingers over the seal.

"Not good enough for you, Hugh? You can't just enjoy it like everyone else?"

"Is everything ok?" Liana touched his elbow but Hugh didn't react.

"I should just go," he said.

"You just got here, don't go yet."

"Let him go," Kain said. "This obviously isn't up to his standards."

"Stop acting like a prick." Hugh said, trying to make himself heard over the sound system. Kain stepped closer, now within the border of the usual personal space given in conversation. Hugh could smell the drink on his breath. He kept his eyes on Hugh as he returned his attention to the packet in his hands and drew out a couple of cigarettes. He stuck one between his lips and held the other out to Hugh.

"Come stand outside with me." He offered patting his pockets down looking for his lighter. Hugh looked at the cigarette that was balancing in the light hold of Kain's slender fingers. Liana was still watching them both, her drink forgotten.

"I'm leaving." Hugh said, but it was so quiet that only Kain caught his words. All Liana saw was his mouth move before he turned and drifted away through the crowded house. Hugh got to the doorway and found that it blocked by the same people. He didn't slip past this time, instead barging through as if he did not see them. The shouts came, but they were behind him now, and the fresh air and space worked at once to ease his anger. He got onto the main road and thought he was alone until Liana's shouts rang out from behind. She called for him to wait. He slowed but only a little as she caught up with him, the click of her heels on the pavement sounding her approach.

"Hugh! Where are you going?" she asked. He stopped and turned to her, struck by the disparity in her beauty and the ugliness of the surroundings.

"It's not my scene, you enjoy yourself. I'm going home."

"Screw the party then. We can do something different, chill at mine if you like. Anything you want."

"Honestly, I just want to get back. Message me tomorrow and we can do something."

"Are you sure?"

"Yeah. Get back to your friends." And with that, Hugh continued walking. Liana walked back to the house over the cracked paving and through the gathered that were smoking. Kain waited at the door, watching.

By the time Hugh reached the summit of his drive he knew

he had returned to the world of silence and solitude. The night was quiet. The sky was now calm and scattered with stars. He placed a hand around the brass knob of the door and ceased to move. It had been less than an hour since he'd left the house and Dylan's film would still be underway inside. He looked toward the woods, from here all he saw was the black peak of trees against the sky. They held a dark appeal. They offered a kind of purpose, a place to be. He would see if it was as empty as he had always known it of anything living that didn't melt away at your approach. He walked to it with long, loping strides down the path he had made, cushioned with flattened grass at his feet and hidden either side by the tall sentry of stems. They dragged against the leg of his jeans and pulled at the cuff of his shirt.

Under the cover of the trees where strange noises sounded from untraceable directions, he turned down the path that cut to the river. He stepped into the clearing expecting to see nothing, but to his surprise the horse was there, stood in the river with the water breaking against her knees. She looked to be resting, but raised her head at his appearance. All thoughts of the party were forgotten. He watched her closely as he crossed the dry ground toward the river.

He stopped, seeing the horse break into motion and wade to the bank, mounting its low slope with ease and continuing to come towards him. Her head was low and her ears forward, approaching with casual interest until they were facing each other within touching distance. The horse raised her head to catch his scent, and he froze as he felt her hot breath coat his hair for a few seconds before she looked back to the water. He extended a hand and placed it against her skin, devoid of warmth. The mare pawed the ground as if restless, nudging his shoulder as if expecting him to do something. Hugh didn't know how to react, continuing with both hands to stroke her coat and trying to discern if she liked it.

To his surprise, the shoulder he'd been stroking began to sink, and he watched her lower her front end to the ground, her rear end hanging in the air for a moment before dropping to the floor with an audible thud. Hugh was unsure what to do. The mare turned to look at him and tossed her head, asking for something in a language he didn't understand. He reached out and touched her sleek skin again in hope this was what she sought, however the horse was still showing signs of agitation, pointing her muzzle behind her and then looking at Hugh with imploring eyes. He placed his other hand behind her wither, applying the slightest pressure and expecting a reaction. She watched him still. He took a rallying breath and lifted a leg over her back where she lay, as gently as he could. He paused before lowering his weight onto her to sit. Her reaction was instantaneous. She rocked backwards; her extended front legs drawing themselves inwards and getting a good footing on the loose ground. Hugh grasped a fistful of mane as he clung to her. She stood in one smooth motion, and at once headed to the river she had come from. Hugh watched the impending rush of shallow water not realising the horse's intentions before it descended the bank and entered the black water. He felt dizzy, hunched forward and seeing only the swirling river far beneath the horse's sloping shoulder. It crept up her lower legs as she waded further in. He felt an abstract terror grip his body and his knees clamped to her sides as the damp crept through his best jeans. His fingers entwined in her mane as he lay helpless across her back. She started to paw and scrape at the water.

Back on dry land, hidden by the heavy cover of trees and vegetation, a figure moved from where they had been standing watch a short distance away. Breath rasped from between old, cracked lips as stubbed fingers split the leaves for a better view. In the water, the horse turned on its hindquarters, dragging her nose through the surface. Hugh had no idea what she was doing. He was an unwitting passenger astride her back, praying silently for their return to dry land. Distracted by his situation, he'd failed to observe the surrounding area, not noticing the man that was watching them from the clearing.

It was only when he heard a faint chuckle carried on the delicate breeze, almost forgettable if it hadn't been for the rough undertone, its origin strange and unfamiliar. It was the kind of sound that knocks you from ease to anxiety at its first utterance, and this was its effect. Hugh's wide eyes darted to locate the source, but before he could make out the dark shapes on land, the world seemed to shift away from him and he found himself mercy to gravity. He plunged into the river as the horse dropped to her knees and rolled on to her side. He scrambled to his feet, his breath knocked from him with the sudden immersion in cold water, but he managed to just about dodge the upended animal whose legs were kicking and creating a splash.

His feet waterlogged and his shirt ruined and stuck to his skin, he escaped the water before addressing the strange noise he'd heard. In the dim space he could make out the shape of a person standing a few feet away. They were short, their hunched silhouette appeared to be smiling, perhaps the same leer from which the alarming laugh had emerged. The horse emerged from the water next to him and made a soft throaty sound, walking towards the figure quite at ease.

The man's voice broke the still that had set over them.

"She likes you it seems. But be thankful that water was shallow." He laughed again, at his first breath it morphed into a coughing fit.

Hugh froze, trying to pick out details of the stranger he was alone with. The man was old, his voice hoarse and his posture poor. A paunch around his middle hung over the string that had tied his trousers. He wore scrappy, bound leather shoes that didn't look in the least bit comfortable, and atop his head a lumpy, woolen cap shadowed his face.

As the man recovered, his hand rose to caress the mare's muzzle. All Hugh noticed was the shape of four pale fingers in the light of the clearing.

"Don't you, Sanna? You like him." he said, this time addressing the horse before lowering his deformed hand and returning his gaze to the boy. "I won't hurt you if that's what you're worried about." His tone was awkward and impatient.

Hugh tried to clear his throat to speak, but the sound was too abrupt.

"I didn't know she was yours."

The old man seemed to consider something for a moment, and then to Hugh's great relief he relaxed and began to assemble a fresh fire within the remains of the previous one, using what burdened his deep pockets. Once finished he sat on a rotted log, pulling it closer to the burgeoning flames.

"She doesn't belong to me, she doesn't belong to anyone. We are old friends." he said, sounding weary. He seemed to search Hugh with his piercing, faintly luminescent eyes. Hugh avoided eye contact, he was trying and failing to think of an excuse to leave without seeming rude. As he processed the words of his new company, questions sprung to the forefront of his mind. He shivered, his wet clothes clinging to his goose touched skin.

"Come sit boy. I bet you're frozen cold, how about I fetch a towel?" The man spoke with a strong accent; it was not native. He hadn't time to answer the suggestion before the man bustled back to the trees, disappearing from sight before he reappeared bearing a brown towel. The horse he called Sanna stood swishing her tail by the water's edge. He wrapped it round his shoulders. Despite the strong smell of mildew and the outdoors it went some way to warming him, and with the fire crackling and beginning to radiate heat, he responded to the man's motioning and sat upon his own log.

"My name's Gamel if you wanted to know," the man said.

"I'm Hugh. Do you live here?" He looked towards the area from where Gamel had retrieved a towel but saw no erected shelter. "In the woods?"

"Yes, for the time being. It's not where we want to be, but Sanna is unwell and too weak to keep moving around. I fear if I move her much further she will cease to move entirely."

Hugh looked again to the horse that to his knowledge was the picture of health.

"What's wrong with her? Would a vet help? I could get you the number."

"No. No vet," Gamel said, and seemed to undergo an inner conflict on whether to say more "We have come a long way, looking for a safe and permanent home. It's been hard for her. She's not accustomed to travelling." Hugh nodded and looked toward the mare with renewed curiosity.

"Where are you from?" Hugh asked. "You don't have to tell me," He added as an afterthought. Gamel watched him with watery, sunken eyes.

"Our original home? That's a long way from here. We're both from Denmark; we lived on a farm there. After the family that owned it moved away, we had to leave. It was to be developed." He spat the last word as if it were bitter on his tongue. "Are you warmed up?" Hugh nodded, but his shivering was beyond his control. "You need to change into some dry clothes."

Hugh got to his feet.

"I don't have far to get home."

"That's good."

"Will you be staying here?"

"For now, most likely. But if you go telling people and they come looking, we'll be gone."

"I won't." Hugh replied quickly. He took a step towards home before Gamel's voice stopped him one last time.

"If you wanted to do me a favour boy, there is something that I'd like."

"What is it?"

"Bring me some salted porridge, a pat of butter on top. You bring that every evening and just leave it by this log and I'll return the favour."

Hugh gave a sincere nod. The rational part of his mind told him it was dangerous, reckless even to get involved with a strange man living rough in the woods. But his encounters with the horse and now the man had been one of his few sources of enjoyment in recent times, and his sole source of excitement. Plus, if it was an excuse to get out of his house and away from the atmosphere of his mother, then even better.

"Should I bring anything for Sanna? I offered her an apple the other day, but she didn't seem to like it."

Gamel's face, lit up in a curious way by the slim reach of the moonlight through the trees and the flicker of the firelight began to move; deep etched, cavernous lines started to shift to accommodate a smile. He was trying to stifle a laugh.

"You won't have much luck feeding her fruit." His smile faded. Hugh said a quick goodbye before heading towards home. As soon as he reached the main path, he ran.

Chapter 5

The following day, Hugh set about his usual routine of dressing and dealing with Dylan. But he had something new now to occupy his thoughts, for his imagination was alight with the memory of how the horse felt beneath him, and his encounter with the man. He'd been trusted with a favour. He knew that any adult would advise against it, but as he sat through the repetitive children's shows trying to face the mess of housework and clutter, he shut his eyes, closing out the house and wishing he was in the trees beyond the garden.

He had a tried and tested method of dealing with household chores. It was the one he found most efficient and requiring the least effort. He shut out all the minor tasks, the ones that didn't affect day to day functioning such as sweeping, mopping, polishing; all that was forgotten. It was the stuff that if you left, it became increasingly difficult to go about your everyday life, and he had tried. Experience told him that when the side and the sink began to fill with dirty cups and plates to the extent that there was no free space on which to prepare any food, that was the time to load the dishwasher. And when the laundry basket would hold no more and the floor became a mire of undistinguishable, musty cotton folds, it was time to use the washing machine. He did what he had to. It was hard sometimes when it felt like all Dylan and his mother did was work against him and create more mess, but he kept things going. As long as Dylan was clothed and fed, that was enough. But he longed for it not to be a burden on his mind and missed the days where he could invite his friends round without worry.

The day was already a bad one. A constant drizzle had persisted and the murky clouds that hung before the sun would send an occasional strong gust of wind, throwing sharp rain against the windows like finger taps. It meant staying indoors and as a result Dylan had been restless and difficult to entertain. After he'd finished serving up packet pasta, eating his portion from the pan and then discarding it on the counter to form its impermeable crust, his mother made an appearance.

They swapped short bursts of small talk in the kitchen, Hugh reluctant, his mother half asleep as he checked the back of the cupboard for porridge oats. Despite his pre-dinner effort, the counter was still chaotic with all variety of mess and items that were not where they belonged. His mother mumbled that she would have to go out and pick up some dinner before she straightened and her eyes cast over the used plate on the slip of free table and the pans and empty instant pasta packets that had spilt their powder residue. He left her by herself.

A few hours later, with Dylan settled and quiet and his mother in the living room, Hugh prepared the porridge. In a short space of time, he'd created a steaming, stodgy mixture, complete with the addition of a scrape of butter on top. It was earlier than yesterday, the sun setting in a vibrant sky that had purged itself of moisture. His thoughts scattered as he walked through the wild lawn, his mother too consumed to notice his strange activity. He'd given no thought to covering the bowl, and so had to hurry as the heat escaped in rising wisps of steam. He mused over the prospect of seeing the man in a brighter setting, without the cover of night. In the heart of the woods, however, he found he hadn't taken into account the extent to which the trees blocked the light. And so, disheartened, he found himself again in a dim clearing, unable to make out any reasonable distance or detail. There was nobody there. He stood feeling foolish, standing alone in an uninhabited wood holding a bowl of cooling, congealing porridge with no one to receive it. The ashes from the fire and the logs they'd made seats out of were still in the same position, so he was at least reassured that the previous evening had not resulted from a tired and overactive mind.

He waited a little while, hanging about making ruts in the sodden leaf floor and inspecting sticks until the low light morphed to near black and he placed the bowl on the wet ground, too afraid to balance it on a log. It looked like it had set to a solid mass of cold, milk swollen oats. He returned home and went straight to his room.

Acting on faith, he took another bowl of porridge to the clearing the following night. He was unsure if he was doing the right thing, but the empty, scraped bowl and spoon he found by the trees showed that his previous offering had been well received. Whilst he appeared to be alone, he seemed to feel the watch of eyes on his back as he placed it where the last bowl had been. He returned home under the watch of a star strung sky, treading the winding path with his hands shoved deep into the pockets of his jeans. That night he lay on his bed, wondering how many days it would be before he could speak to the old man again and find out if the horse's health was improving. He received a message from Liana for the first time since the night of the party, asking him how he was. He had little interest in conversation, but heard without probing that it had been a great party. There was no regret.

The next day Hugh woke unaware that anything was out of the ordinary. Through bleary, sleep encrusted eyes he followed Dylan downstairs on weary legs without paying attention to the accustomed to mess. On Dylan's insistence he went to the kitchen to make him a drink, but as he pushed open the door, all drowsiness disappeared in surprise at what he saw. The entire kitchen and dining area was tidy and clean. The worktop which yesterday had been a commotion of wrappers, food scraps and dirty dishes was now a clear, shiny surface. It was so rare that he saw more than a small space of the patterned counter top that it appeared strange and new. His mother was still upstairs, undoubtedly asleep. He wondered if she had experienced some kind of surge of energy late last night before retiring to her bed. However it had happened, he was just grateful for some space to prepare breakfast.

The sun was high and bright outside. They made what they could of it, dressed in shorts and t-shirts in the back garden space. Hugh joined in Dylan's play when required, sat and watched when he could. The air was balmy, thick with busy insects and the far travelling sounds of lawnmowers and vocal birds. Inside his mother slept the day away, either unable or unwilling to fill it with anything other than the blackness of her half-conscious mind.

Later in the day, Hugh was making a drink when the sound of sudden excitement from Dylan signaled his mother's appearance. She had dressed but still looked to be continuing her streak of not washing. She wrapped her arms around Dylan, who had secured himself to her legs upon sight, but her face looked shocked as she took in the kitchen.

"Did you do this Hugh?" she asked with breathless surprise. Hugh struggled for a reply, floundering at the fact she herself was not responsible. "It looks lovely in here, thank you." She ran her fingers over the side and flicked the kettle on. She looked and sounded as though tears were close, and Hugh had not the heart to say anything that would bring them on or raise any concern. If it had not been his mother, and it wasn't Dylan, there was only one other person who could have done it. He went to leave the room, but on the way out remembered something.

"Can you buy more porridge, please?" Confusion passed

over his mother's face. "Sure, I'll go to the shop tomorrow. I noticed you've been eating it all of a sudden."

"Yeah," he replied, cutting the conversation short.

Later that evening he was back in the woods, warm bowl of porridge in one hand whilst his eyes adjusted to the low light. He had watched from his bedroom window as the sun had given way to gloomy dusk and lights had sprung into existence on both ground and sky. It was a different world out here to the hazy afternoon he had spent relaxing with his brother. The temperature had dropped just enough to be cold without a thin jacket to cover his arms. He saw Sanna straight away, stood with a back hoof propped at an angle in rest. Her mane and tail was combed and braided to the very end.

As he walked to take a seat on one of the logs, Gamel came forwards from the leafy shadows, his distinctive cap and wooden gait making him easy to identify. The man's sunken eyes shone from within the pale moon of his face and his skin showed the many marks of old age; a leathery network of deep crevices, dotted with blemishes and growths of every shape and shade of brown. He hunched forward, his shoulders almost meeting the faded red cap. It gave the impression that his head was slowly sinking into his ailing body. Gamel lurched to a log and sat down, taking the bowl from Hugh and tucking into the warm oats. Hugh couldn't help staring at the disfigured hands that held the bowl and used the spoon. The knuckle joints were hideously swollen and each of his four fingers thick and unwilling to bend.

It wasn't long before Gamel had finished eating and set the bowl down. Hugh heard Sanna approach them. His discomfort grew as she reached him. She towered over him and made him feel small. Her head began to bob, and she picked at the ground with her hooves.

"Leave him be old girl." Gamel said in a scolding tone. Hugh reached out a hand for her to smell and she settled as she inhaled his scent. She seemed placid enough until her ears turned away and she lunged at him as if to bite.

"Pah!" Gamel shouted and chased her with his hands. She trotted back to the river where she contented with standing and shooting the occasional brooding look toward the pair. Gamel looked Hugh over and a slight smile softened his face, easing his anxiety. "Don't mind her lad. She's been restless lately."

"It's fine," he replied. "I like her."

"You just be careful around her." Hugh nodded and Gamel continued. "Thank you for the porridge; it's been just what I needed. I feel much stronger."

"I'm glad to help. Did you-" he paused, feeling over his words. "Did you clean the kitchen?" he asked, trying to gauge the old man's reaction. "I have to ask, because it wasn't me or my mum."

"I did," Gamel said with a grave expression. "Is that ok?"

"Yeah, it's great thank you. You didn't have to do that though."

"I always repay any favour owed. It's part of the morals I live by," Gamel said. Hugh nodded his head, his lips a zipped seal.

"How did you get in the house?" Hugh felt bold, intrusive, which by manner of his question was ironic; He was asking how an acquaintance had entered his own house while his family had been asleep. Gamel smirked.

"Through the bloody door lad, how else would I get in?" Hugh smiled but breathed an internal sigh of relief. He made a mental note to check the locks before bed. If there was one thing his mother wasn't usual careless with, it was the locks. "Your mor's not particularly attentive is she?"

"She spends most of her time in bed. Have you had any luck

finding somewhere to live?"

"It's complicated."

"Can I help in any way?" he asked, and Gamel looked at him with a guarded expression. In his pocket a gnarled finger tightened around a crumpled and heavily degraded piece of paper that had been thumbed countless times.

"I'm not even sure where we're heading now. I seem to have lost my bearings," he said, and a quiet moment of reflection passed between them.

"What was it like where you used to live?"

"It was a big, thatched farmhouse, right out in the country. It had a lake, with ducks and willows at one end. That's where I met Sanna." Gamel broke off and began to cough. His chest wheezed in the breaths he drew trying to recover.

"I've always lived here," Hugh said. "My dad used to live with us before he left." Hugh dropped his gaze, and it fell upon Gamel's hands. The old man noticed his change in focus and slipped them back into the wide pockets of his dark cord trousers.

"You've not told anyone we're here, as I asked?"

"No," he said, shaking his head. Gamel reached into the knapsack he'd placed on the ground and brought out a woolen blanket; it looked stiff with age and exposure to the outdoors. He offered it to Hugh, who politely declined. Gamel wrapped it around his legs for warmth.

"I miss my home, but I knew I had to leave. In the modern world, I have no place there. Sanna's future was bleak and I couldn't leave her behind. So we've been travelling ever since. It's not been easy but we're both still together, that's what's important. She's all I have."

Hugh looked at the horse who was resting as she stood. The water coursed around her strong, slender legs and her head drooped, shielded by dripping plaits of mane.

"Sometimes I think," Gamel continued, "maybe it wasn't the right thing. We're still without a home, and this country hasn't been all that was promised." His hidden hand clenched around the crumpled paper. "Sometimes I think we're not meant to have a future."

"Maybe I can help." Hugh said. Gamel looked at him with a hopeful expression. "I can see what houses are for sale or rent." He glanced at Gamel's boots held loosely at the seams and his patched jacket. All his possessions seemed to be held within a single knapsack. "Or I can help look for locations nearby. What is it you're looking for?"

"A building of some sort, shelter, it doesn't need to be big. I can make modifications. It has to be remote enough to ensure our safety, and there needs to be water, deeper the better." Hugh thought it over, he presumed the old man had no money or accustom to conventional living, but the requirement for deep water struck him as strange.

"Will Sanna need anything?"

"She's who the water's for." Gamel smirked, the expression warping his face. Hugh had countless questions buzzing through his mind, but felt too intimidated by the Gamel's bluntness to ask them. He had next to no knowledge about the world outside his own, let alone horses. He let it rest.

"Ok, I can try looking on Google Maps to see what there is." Gamel raised an eyebrow.

"You'd be better off handing a map to me, lad."

"Oh, no I meant on the computer."

"The what?" Gamel's eyes traced Hugh's face in suspicion.

"A computer; it's a kind of device which has lots of information on it."

Gamel's eyebrows were raised so high that the skin they displaced in deep ridges threatened to swallow them from existence.

"A physical map, that's what you want lad. That has information on where things are located."

"Yeah, that's what I'm talking about. Except on the computer it's one big picture they've taken from the sky. You can zoom in close and see exactly what's there, and I can get a better idea of whether places are any good before going there."

Hugh expected him to be impressed. Instead, Gamel had raised his eyes to the night sky and was studying it intently with guarded fear.

"Trust me. I can have a good luck at the nearby area without you or Sanna having to go anywhere." he said. Gamel dropped his gaze back to the boy who hoped he trusted him.

"If I'm honest, I don't much like the sound of it. But I'll take your word. Go on home; you look like you could do with some rest." Hugh stood and brushed off the gathered wood dirt and lichen. Now that he was on his feet, he could feel the fatigue that weighted his muscles.

"I'll see you soon then," he said as he left. Gamel stayed seated until the retreating image of Hugh's jacketed back disappeared behind the tree line.

Chapter 6

The following two evenings, Hugh took porridge to the clearing without seeing Sanna or Gamel. The overnight cleaning continued. On waking he would notice another area cleaned or tidied, despite his vigilance in checking the locks each night. His mother noticed too, but presumed Hugh had taken a sudden interest in domestic upkeep, and as they rarely spoke he didn't have to attempt any explanation or feign responsibility.

A new issue was the diminishing supply of oats. By the third night, there were not enough left to make a bowl. Hugh tried to rouse his mother after lunch and ask her to get more. She responded enough to tell him through half-closed eyes and a dry mouth that she would get some when she went out. She had kicked away the cover and wiped at her face, reaching for the water perched on the bedside table next to three other used cups and stacks of old books. Hugh didn't have the patience to wait at the door, but downstairs his waiting met no end.

The evening came and passed and night was settling in by the time Hugh's mother finally appeared at the foot of the stairs in her bedclothes. Hugh was restless, worrying about having no food to take to Gamel. But he had taken it daily for a week now so thought one night wouldn't matter. It bothered him enough that he followed his mother to the kitchen to talk. He found her stood in the centre of the room, pivoting on her feet and looking about herself as if confused. She looked awful. She gave a start at his entry.

"Oh Hugh, did Dylan get some dinner?"

"Yes," he replied, thinking of the scrambled eggs he had made for him. The plates, pan and discarded egg shells were spread around either side of the hob.

"Thank you," she said, rubbing at her forehead.

"Are you going to the shop?" he asked her, his mother glanced at the clock.

"It's a bit late for that. What do you need?"

"Porridge, I keep telling you."

"Oh yes. You did ask me. I'll go tomorrow I promise. I'll get some meals in too. I was thinking of making some pasta, do you want some with me?"

Hugh reluctantly answered that he did. He didn't enjoy spending time around his mother but it was too hard to turn down a cooked meal.

Half an hour later, Hugh and his mother sat at the table and ate the tuna pasta she'd made in silence. To Hugh it tasted divine. He was still sidetracked by the old man out in the woodland. He thought of going to explain, but the rain that lashed at the windows was enough to put him off. He'd hold out until the next day.

His sleep came to an abrupt end when he found himself upright in a split second. A great banging and clattering reverberated through the house in stark contrast to the easy dawn outside. He wasn't the only one to hear it, as two loud thumps and the creak of a door signaled both the awakening and movement of his mother. The jarring noise halted, and Hugh reasoned he should also get up and investigate. He descended the stairs. Behind him, Dylan poked his head around his door, looking dazed. He could hear his mother in the kitchen.

"Hugh?" she called. Hugh answered with his entrance and saw what had been the source of all the commotion.

"What on earth have you been doing in here?" she asked, crouching down to the floor. Hugh rubbed sleep from his eyes. The kitchen had been messy when he'd gone to bed, scattered with the days used utensils and empty packets, but now it was trashed. The contents of the cupboard had been pulled out and spread about the sides like spewed up guts. The fridge was open, disemboweled. The interior light was on in answer to the sudden, extended demand and yoghurts and milk had tumbled out on to the floor, some splitting and spilling to add to the mess. He saw what must have caused the great clattering. A large assortment of pots and pans were lying now silent on the dirty tiled floor. It seemed they had fallen from the counter.

"What possessed you to do this? It's just about every pan we own. Did you make a great pile of them or something?" His mother ran a trembling hand through her hair and looked shaken. Dylan watched in the doorway.

"I don't know. I don't remember it, maybe I was sleepwalking," he said, feeling guilty for not having checked the locks before he'd gone to bed.

With nothing more to say, he left his mother and returned to his room. Dylan followed at his heels.

"Did you really do that, Hugh? What's sleepwalking? How do you not remember?" Hugh did his best to ignore his little brother, but when he sat on his bed, Dylan rushed to him and persisted with his questions.

"Shush! I need to think," he shouted. Immediate guilt hit him for raising his voice. Dylan quietened, distracted by the view from the window. Hugh cradled his head and closed his eyes.

When the afternoon came and his mother still hadn't been to the shops, Hugh sent a text to Liana. It was a five minute walk from the bottom of his drive to reach the new build estate within which Liana lived; he only had to turn right rather than left at the footpath. It was strange to go from the wild sprawl of greenery and nature that surrounded his own home to the manicured shrubs and regiment length turf that did little to separate the shoebox houses here. She opened the door and invited him in.

"I've been worried about you since the other night," she said, leading him into the kitchen where she leant against an immaculate breakfast bar. "You left in such a hurry."

"It's no big deal. You see now why I don't go to those things."

"It's a shame. I don't know why Kain was acting like that." She offered him a drink, but he declined, watching as she poured herself a glass of filtered water before setting it down on the bare counter next to them. "Are you sure you're ok?"

"Fine, thanks. I need to ask you for something though."

"Sure, what d'you need?"

"It's going to sound weird, but my mum won't go to the shops and I haven't got any money. I need some porridge oats."

"What?" Liana laughed. "I think we have the sachets, would they be ok?"

"Yeah."

She retrieved a box of porridge sachets from a cupboard. He avoided her bemused expression.

"You know I'm always here if you want anything. You can tell me if there's something wrong," she said.

"Thank you, everything's ok though."

"Have you seen any more of that horse?" He moved towards the door, biting down on his lip.

"No, it must have been a one off."

"You can stay longer if you want; my parents are both at work."

"I've got to get back, thanks again though for your help. I appreciate it." He paused by the door, thinking for a moment. "Perhaps I could use your internet sometime? I don't have it at home."

"Sure, you don't want to use it now?"

"Another day, I'll message you."
"Ok. Bye then. Remember what I said."

That evening, he went to the woods again. Alone, when no one else was awake, he sought company. At the clearing, Sanna lay by the water. Her head was low as if in deep repose and she remained still even at his approach. With slow, deliberate steps he got within a meter of her and dropped to the ground, kneeling and then sitting with his hand outstretched. Her head bobbed. She seemed to appraise him with the one black, depthless eye that he could see. He moved closer, and she turned to him. She took in his smell with shallow breaths, the length of her mane trailing in the dirt.

"It's me," Hugh said, his voice a mere whisper in the dark. "I'm won't hurt you."

Sanna's head dropped to meet his hand. His palm rested between her eyes where her forelock split into strands, taking care not to startle her. In this way, with Hugh touching first her head and forelock, then moving to feel her mane and the broad muscle of her shoulder, they spent a length of time. His contact remained light and cautious, always watching her for signs of agitation or unrest. There was nothing else, no care or concern, even if Gamel observed from a nearby tree. The sight and feel of the horse immersed him.

After a time, when the cold had crept into his limbs and the dampness of the ground through his trousers, he withdrew his hand. He stood up and took a step back. Sanna tossed her head and also began to move. Drawing her legs out and in front of her she stood, shaking off the leaves and debris that clung to her coat. She turned from him and went to the water, entering without hesitation. Hugh left without a goodbye.

Chapter 7

The pan boiled over on the hob top, spilling white frothy water over its sides in alarming swathes. Hugh turned off the gas and watched it settle. Although the water had subsided, the hob was now covered in a wet, salty sheen. He prodded a wooden spoon into it to inspect the damage. It met with an almost solid block of overcooked pasta, which he scraped off the bottom of a pan and into a colander to drain. They'd run out of sauce jars, so he added a jar of chopped, cold tomatoes over the pasta and stirred it in.

"Is dinner ready yet?" Dylan asked from the doorway.

"Just about," he replied. He added some remnants of mixed herbs and enough grated cheese to make it palatable.

"It's a bit lumpy." Dylan said as they sat at the table five minutes later.

"Just eat around the tomatoes if you don't like them."

Hugh had just finished stacking the bowls onto the washing up pile when his mum entered the kitchen, groggy with sleep. She mumbled something about dinner and had a quick look at the pots left on the stove. Hugh skirted round her and headed to his room before she noticed the new block of cheese now half its size.

When his mother was once again settled in her chair, progress from the bed, he rooted around for a clean bowl and prepared the porridge. He shrugged on a light jacket and left the house, closing the door on the sound of his mother's television show and stepping across the dewy grass towards the tree line. There was little light to guide him; a heavy cover of cloud and a slip of moon made the evening darker than usual. But the path was familiar and when he was close enough, he could make out that black entrance between the trunks.

His breathing was heavy and jarring in the quiet, but it wasn't long before he could hear the river. The recent rainfall had swollen it. It seemed louder than usual, rushing over the rocky ground with an amplified presence. He scanned the trees for Gamel but saw nothing other than bark and leaves. He considered trying to find him but decided against it. The night was cold and barren. He knew if Gamel wanted his company he would make himself known, so he left the bowl in its usual position, hoping it wouldn't cool too much.

The following day Hugh decided that he would wait as long as it took to see Gamel that evening. He packed a blanket, a spare hoodie, some snacks and a thermos of hot tea to take with him, along with the customary porridge. With his blanket underneath him and the extra layer covering his arms and back, he was at peace as he sat watching the river in the last light of the day. Once he'd remained still for a few minutes, the birds resumed their lively evening serenade, and high above the expanse of leaves concealed both sky and humanity.

The light continued to fade and in front of him the water darkened. Even the birds quieted as they hid away for the night. Hugh sipped on the thermos until there was no more tea and it had cooled in his hands. Cramp began to set in his legs and the sounds of the nighttime woodland were mere background. He heard the shuffle of approaching boots and saw Gamel's outline passing through the trees. He sat next to Hugh and grunted in his direction as he took the bowl and tried to stir through the now congealed oats. Gamel grunted again, but this time in displeasure. It didn't stop him eating it all and scraping the bowl.

"Sorry about missing a night," Hugh said, putting the empty flask on the ground. "We ran out of oats, I didn't forget. My mum hasn't been shopping."

"Is there something wrong with your mor?"

"She's ill," he said, looking away. "She has been for a long time. I got some off a friend."

"Thanks lad, it's much appreciated."

"It was you who messed up the kitchen wasn't it, and knocked the pans over."

"I got angry. I can't help it sometimes, when my temper takes hold and I don't think very clearly."

"If I don't come, it's because I can't. I wouldn't do it to upset you."

There was a low snort from the direction of the river, and Sanna now stood there. Gamel was eyeing up his blanket.

"I know what it's like to have no help." Gamel said.

"Don't you have any family where you used to live?"

"No. Sanna's all I have." He was quiet for a moment. "I'll see if I can improve things at home for you," Gamel began. But Hugh cut him off.

"You don't have to, we can manage by ourselves."

"I know I don't have to, but you weren't listening when I said, I know what it's like, to feel like you're on your own." Gamel was facing him with a watery stare. "I've been around for a long time, and during that time I've made a point of living by some simple rules. One of them is that if someone helps me, I return the favour. That's not going to change." Hugh nodded, wide eyed.

"Hopefully I can bring some meat in a couple of days."

"That'd be great. I'm worried about Sanna."

"Is the meat for her?"

"What would you say if it was?" Hugh didn't reply. "It's curious, the way she is with you. Are you scared of her?"

"A little."

"You should be."

Sanna was no longer in the river. Hugh pulled out his phone and checked the time, Gamel's words sticking in his mind. It was late.

"I'm going to head home. Do you want this?" he offered Gamel his blanket, who took it in his hands with a kind of reverence. It was far softer than his old one.

"Dylan, wait!" Hugh called. He picked up a jog to keep his younger brother in sight. Dappled light danced on the thin cotton of Dylan's disappearing back as he ran as fast as his short legs could carry him. He jumped over the protruding roots that crossed the path, laughing every time Hugh shouted for him to slow. He rounded the corner and saw Dylan in the clearing, waiting for him at last.

"Let's make a den," Dylan said.

"Sure." He caught his breath. "We need to find the right tree and some branches." They began looking. It wouldn't be hard to think of ways he'd rather spend his Saturday, but he had patience for Dylan, especially because he was his brother's only friend.

They picked through fallen branches and nettle patches until they found the right spot well hidden from the path. Dylan danced as Hugh propped up a large branch against a tree, nestling it in the trunk's split.

"More branches!" he said. "We need lots more, keep going."

"You going to help me?" Hugh was scanning the ground for more sticks. "I can't do it on my own."

After a time of content gathering and building, the den was made. It was early afternoon by the time they were back home and taking off their shoes.

Their mother came downstairs, fresh out of the shower. Hugh barely looked in her direction, but Dylan wrapped his little arms around her legs like a vice. She cuddled him for a brief moment then listened to him tell her about their new den. The day passed and Dylan stayed next to his mum's side, following her around like a loyal dog each time she moved, settling by her side each time she sat. Dylan put on his favourite film to show her. After twenty minutes she was out cold. The light in his eyes dimmed, but he was still happy to be held.

That evening, Hugh was in his bedroom when his door creaked ajar, spilling light from the hallway into his bedroom. His mother looked in at him and he sat upright on his bed.

"Hey, I wanted to speak to you," she said. She sounded exhausted.

"What is it?"

"I just wanted to say I'm sorry for being out of it so much lately. I know it's not fair on you." She waited for a reply. Hugh turned his attention back to his phone. "I've made an appointment with the doctor tomorrow to get some medication. I'll try to get sorted properly this time."

Minutes passed in the dark quiet of the bedroom.

"I love you," she said. He listened to the soft padding of her slippers as she retreated from his room and down the corridor.

Hugh covered up in his hand-me-down coat that, although too big, would keep him warm. His tread was slippy as he trekked towards the trees. An encore of rainfall had slicked the long grass whilst they'd been in. Summer was in full flow and the young leaves on the branches cast a bright and hopeful new colour in the day, but by night they gave a new volume to the woodland and every gust of wind set the leaves moving, each separate to each other, taking on a life of their own as if the wind breathed a very soul and with it, animation into those thousands of green extensions up above. He looked back over his shoulder at the house every few steps. He didn't want Dylan to follow him. Before he'd left, his brother had asked him where he went each night. Hugh had distracted him with a film he wouldn't usually be allowed to watch, and when Dylan was occupied with this and some of Hugh's highly prized corner shop sweets, he slipped out of the back door.

He couldn't shake the chill that had gripped his mind the night before. He was working hard to prevent his thoughts from darkening with fear. He kept his eyes fixed on the path, afraid of what he might see either side in those dark, damp hiding places. At the clearing, he saw Sanna straight away. She stood in the shallows of the river like a water feature, pale white and motionless. She faced him, her head slightly lowered and her sides rising and falling with steady breathing. Her eyelids drooped in a dreamy, heavy way and the rest of her stood like a white stone carving watching him silent in the night.

The sound of snapping sticks and things being thrown was coming from nearby, interspersed with furious cursing. It was Gamel. Hugh headed towards the noise, bowl held out in front of him in hope of appeasement. As he got closer, he realised it was where he and his brother had played earlier in the day.

"Bloody mess it is, a bleedin' rock! What's that supposed to be, a bleedin' pillow? Blinding hovel fit for a goat, if that!"

Hugh stepped with care towards the den that he and his brother had built. Sticks and branches were tossed aside, part dismantling the outer structure. He got to the opening where the makeshift signage Dylan had proudly erected was pushed over, ground flat into the grime of the dirt and the wet, fallen leaves. He ducked his head to look inside, still with the food offering held in his hand. Just as he opened his mouth to speak, a rock flew past his head, displaced air shaving his earlobe. It landed with a heavy thump behind him.

"Watch out," he said. A bent figure shuffled around in the tight space to face him.

"Ah, you've made an appearance. What do you call this shoddy attempt at crafting?"

"That rock almost hit me you know."

Gamel breezed straight past him making a "pah" sound with his lips and a dismissive push with his hands. He wheeled round to face him again with a sudden alertness.

"That for me?" he asked, reaching for the bowl as he spoke. Hugh passed it over without a word. He watched Gamel prop up the nearest log to sit on and eat. It took a few noisy mouthfuls before he spoke again.

"I was just trying to clear out some of the junk left lying around in there."

"It wasn't junk. It's a den I helped my brother build earlier."

Gamel paused his eating to give Hugh a look that said it was not a subject to argue over with him. Hugh sighed and moved his feet to keep warm.

"I suggest you find a more worthwhile way to spend your free time," Gamel grunted.

"No luck finding a home yet then?"

"Not any. I've been roughing it in some decrepit tent I can barely lay down in. Sanna won't move further than about a mile each way if I try to look."

"Why ?"

"She wants to stay where she feels safe, maybe?" He shrugged. "Maybe she's still weak, either way she's decided to pay no mind to what I think we should do."

Sanna's eyes brightened and she stepped through the water to the bank, making it look like a great effort on tired limbs. She approached them, throwing her head out and then in again with every step. Gamel placed a rough, weathered hand across her shoulders and patted.

"She's not stupid," he said.

Sanna was standing with one back hoof propped up against the ground and her bottom lip hanging lower as they spoke. Suddenly her ears flicked forward and her head rose in one smooth movement. She stood perfectly alert to something no one else but she could see or hear until they heard a small voice.

"Hugh?"

Dylan stepped into the clearing with bare, grimy feet, dressed in his nightclothes and looking lost. Hugh looked to where Gamel was standing beside him, except he'd gone. Only Sanna was with him, her body taut with a palpable excitement. He rushed forward towards his brother. Sanna followed with the sound of heavy hoof thuds behind.

"What are you doing here? You're not wearing a coat," he said, dropping level with his brother's face and taking one of his cold hands into his own. He shrugged off his jacket to wrap it around Dylan.

"I couldn't sleep. You weren't in the house, so I came to find you."

"What were you thinking? It's dangerous out here."

Without Gamel the woods had taken on a sinister cloak of unsettling shadows and unnatural quiet. He felt watchful eyes and bated breath from behind every trunk and branch. Even Sanna, who Hugh usually felt safe with, seemed threatening in how she stood so close. Like the way her ever damp fur stuck like slick rubber and her matte black eyes lacked any light.

Dylan's eyes were wide at the sight of her, level with her grey muzzle. Sanna seemed to sense Hugh's suspicion. She extended the charcoal end of her nose, closing the gap between herself and the small boy. Her nostrils flared, flashing hot pink in heavy exhalations as she breathed his smell. Hugh rose and went to step between them, meaning to move Dylan back to the path and towards home. But as soon as he moved, Sanna's head rose so fast that he had to duck to save his own from being hit. He saw her ears pinned flat back against her neck. She struck the ground with her front hooves in and lunged at him, her eyes rolling wildly. Dylan cried out and Hugh tried to back away, keeping himself between the horse and his brother. Sanna arched her neck, making her appear twice her normal size. She moved around to the side of the boys and tried to separate them, spinning her haunches to push Hugh away whilst her front end guided Dylan in the river's direction.

"Hugh, what's happening? I'm scared."

"It's ok," he replied. "Don't panic, just stay away from the water."

He got a grip of his brother. With one hand clasping the loose fabric of Dylan's pyjamas it left only his other to fend off the horse who still lashed out with her teeth and blocked them with her body.

"Move out the way!" he shouted. He flung out his arm as if to strike her and she reacted furiously. Those fast twitching ears flattened beyond view and her eyes like two onyx stones formed in the vesicles of lava, rolled back inside her skull into oblivion as she regressed from a placid, malleable creature into a wild, frothing thing. Her front hooves rose from the ground in temper. Hugh saw them flash past his face and rise ever higher before they made their descent, striking out towards where he and Dylan stood.

He stumbled backwards and pulled his brother back with him hard, out of danger's way. But Dylan's foot hit a protruding rock, stealing his balance and owing him a rough delivery to the ground. He was still crying as he groped blindly for his brother's help. Sanna rushed forward, spinning her hindquarters to face Hugh with two very active back legs. They were only a few feet from the water now, blocked by the angry creature, and Sanna's intentions became clear. She lowered her head and began to shunt Dylan towards the water's edge, prompting hysterics from the young boy.

"Ny!" A loud, rattling voice shouted from somewhere in the trees, seeming to stop everything in motion. The horse's head shot up, listening to the sound. Hugh looked round expecting to see Gamel, but could only make out tree boughs and leafy spaces. He didn't waste time. Whilst Sanna was distracted he scrambled to his feet and picked his brother off the ground. Sanna's attention snapped back to what they were doing. Just as she was about to advance again, the same shout came louder.

"Nyk!"

As the strange, foreign word rang through the woodland space, the horse reacted with a snort and a wild swing of her head as she whirled on the spot and ran into the water, disappearing upstream. The sound of her retreat died down, leaving them alone together in the clearing.

With no time for composure, Hugh hauled his weeping brother off the ground.

"Come on," he urged, unable to hide his desperation, but Dylan needed no encouragement. They fled from that place, tracing the path by memory out of the woods. Every raised root and undulation disappeared beneath them in quick succession until the exit was in view. On approach, slowed down by his brother, Hugh had an awful fear that the deep recesses of the woods would swallow them up, the exit evading them upon approach like a cruel mirage of the night. They would be chased on exhausted legs by strange shouts from stranger shadows, by thundering hooves that churned up the ground like they themselves would be churned upon capture;

and it would never end in pursuit of a dawn that ran with them, never closer, until at its end he would have to come to cease and sit down on shaking legs, but by doing so offer his brother to the capture also. If it were just him, he could succumb without guilt or regret, but the hinge of his fear was held within that cold, mud streaked hand that clasped his with that vulnerability only young children possess.

He squeezed Dylan's hand tighter, afraid to let him go, and with every step the exit drew mercifully closer until at last they were through. Relief rolled through him in a wave, but he didn't dare stop. He could feel his brother lagging by the increased resistance pulling him back. He turned round, breathless.

"Come on Dylan, we can stop when we're inside the house."

"I can't," Dylan wailed, dragging his feet. Hugh wished they could wait, but his view kept being drawn to that black gaping mouth of trees and it terrified him. It was less than a hundred meters to the house. He got alongside Dylan and used his arms to both wrap around him and propel him forwards. His little brother made an awful mewling sound whilst his legs worked to push him forwards. Hugh couldn't help being reminded of the sound a young baby animal makes when it knows not what is wrong, just that something is wrong.

They got to the door. Hugh pushed it open and they tumbled inside. Rather than the warm sanctuary Hugh had been seeking, the house felt as hostile as the world outside. There was nobody waiting for them. He locked the door and led Dylan through the kitchen. The dark corners and black crevices which served as hiding holes for unpleasant creatures made it impossible for him to let go of his twitchiness until he flicked on the light switch. Dylan was a pasty white.

He hugged his brother's shaky frame close to him, trying to soothe him, but he could feel the cold coming from his pale skin and damp clothes.

"Come upstairs. Let's get you dry."

They headed upstairs and on the way past their mother's bedroom he kicked the door ajar, buffered by a dense layer of strewn clothes. The little light =was enough for him to make out she was in bed, unaware of what had happened.

An anger rose within him that he found hard to suppress. His priority was his brother, who trailed after him into the bathroom then stood, lacking the energy to move. Hugh was tight-lipped as he undressed his brother. With a pile of dirty pyjamas now placed on the grimy linoleum, he turned on the shower and lifted his brother in. At first he cried hard as the hot water hit his ivory skin, acclimatised to biting cold. But slowly his shakes subsided and the warm running water quietened him to a sniffle.

He dried and dressed his younger brother, fresh tears only coming when Dylan noticed scratches where grasping branch ends had broken his skin. He switched off the light, pausing at the door when he heard Dylan speak.

"I'm scared," Dylan said. Hugh returned to his bedside.

"Don't say that, don't be scared."

"The horse wanted to hurt me. It wanted you to go so I would be alone with it and that man."

"Did you see a man?" he asked.

"The man that was with you when I came, the small man with funny hands."

Hugh's skin turned cold.

"I know that man, he wouldn't hurt us. He's moving away soon."

"When?"

"I don't know but soon. Don't be scared. Where he's staying is far away from our house, deep in the woods. It's just while he finds somewhere new to live, and then he'll be gone."

"Hugh?"

"What?"

"I think that man is living in the shed," he said with wide eyes.

"Why d'you think that?"

"I saw the shed door open and shut this morning from the window. I thought it was you but then I found out you were in your room."

Hugh tried to hide his fear in front of his brother, but had to reassure himself that he had double bolted the door.

"Don't worry, the doors are locked and you're safe. That man's my friend but tomorrow I'll sort everything out ok? You've got to promise me though that you'll never go into the woods alone again, even if you think I'm in there."

"Ok, I won't."

He looked exhausted but the way he gripped his duvet and the fight left in his eyes told Hugh that sleep would be a while yet. He stood and kissed his brother.

"Get some sleep," he said, leaving the door ajar.

The old farmhouse was entirely at rest, with not even background TV buzz or the inane noises of home activity to warm the empty void. Hugh had long forgone the expectation of such sounds. What he'd been hoping for was some sign of life from his mother. Midway along the upstairs landing he paused at the elongated, single glazed window. His weight fell on one of the lurking creaky floorboards and the noise of it startled him. He pressed his face close to the netting that had seen far better days, not wanting to lift it, squinting as if to pinpoint his aim of sight through one of those tiny diamond gaps and outside across the garden. He made out the shed. It stood inconspicuous, showing no signs of an intruder. He would wait until morning to investigate. With that decided he pulled the curtains closed in one sweep and headed to his mother's room.

He opened the door with his fist, the strewn clothes relenting and allowing him a foot more space to enter. The light transformed the dingy space to an over bright one in absence of a light shade. His mother had instinctively raised a hand to shield her eyes from the painful surge of brightness that had hit. She began to roll from her side onto her back with the slow, considered effort required after a deep sleep.

"Wake up," he said through clenched teeth, still trying to keep his temper under control. He got no response, only a slight twitch of her raised hand. "Wake up!"

"Why was the shower on?" she said. Her words slurred, her mouth not caught up with the requirement to wake.

"Your youngest son left the house and went into the woods alone."

"What?"

"You're lucky he didn't get lost or seriously hurt. You're lucky I was there to bring him back." His words flew out in angry bursts, constrained by the tightness in his chest but amplified when they reached release. He remembered Dylan would still be awake and glanced towards the door. His mother finally took her hand from her eyes and used it to prop herself somewhat upright on the pillows. She seemed to finally understand the meaning of his words. He could almost see them hit her one by one as her brow creased and her chest rose and her red, sleep smothered eyes filled with murky moisture.

"Is he back?"

"He is now. I've put him to bed, not like his own mother would take care of him or even realise he was gone is it?"

"Watch how you speak to me." Her voice trembled as she spoke.

"That's what you're worried about? The way one son speaks

to you after he just saved the other from getting lost outside at night?"

"I-"

"Why don't you get up? Why don't you be a mother?" He was shouting now, all control lost.

"I'm trying Hugh, I'm going to try." His mother sobbed. Like a small child she clutched the duvet like a comforter, pawing at her face with clumsy hands to smear away the tears. He couldn't look at her. He turned away and walked to the door kicking the clutter as he went. He heard the soft collapse of his mother's weight into the mattress. He didn't have to look to know she was gripped in a fetal curl, sinking wetly into self-sorrow.

"Pathetic," he said, slamming the door shut in closure.

He crossed the hall to his own room feeling full of guilt for how loud he had shouted and what Dylan must have heard, but the anger didn't subside. He stormed into his room and stood, chest heaving, every sinew of muscle at full attention and begging for an output. He spun and punched the wall. Hot white pain flashed in his knuckles but it left a satisfying imprint in the now cracked plaster. His breathing was still heavy. He kicked the foot of his bed hard with the toe of his trainers, the pain of a stubbed toe adding to that of his raw knuckles.

He Kicked off his trainers and hobbled to the bathroom to brush his teeth. He splashed his face with cold water and headed back to his bed. He'd just got comfortable when his brother started to cry. He waited to see if their mother would answer him, but after five minutes the cries intensified. He went to Dylan and lay with him. The tears soon stopped, and after a little while both boys fell asleep.

Chapter 8

The morning sun seeped through the unbacked curtains in Dylan's room, waking Hugh at an hour he didn't like to see. His neck and shoulders were stiff from sharing a single bed, yet Dylan wasn't with him.

He knew something was amiss as the television wasn't on. His brother would normally be absorbed in cartoons and waiting to pester him for breakfast, but the living room was quiet and empty and the sound of animated chatter was coming from the kitchen. Dylan was in there, talking to their mother as she loaded the dishwasher.

"Morning," she said. "I've got a doctor's appointment this afternoon, are you ok to watch your brother?"

"You don't usually ask."

"Well hopefully, if it all goes ok then this'll be the last time for a while."

"Whatever," he said, taking his food to the living room.

Dylan resumed his conversation, oblivious to any tension.

Hugh breezed through the kitchen, dumping his bowl and spoon on the newly wiped surface as he passed.

"Where are you going?" Dylan asked, watching him pull his boots on.

"Stay inside."

He left the house out the back door, pulling it shut behind him with a thud. The air was warm and humid, with no clouds to filter the sun's reach. He could hear the low rumble of an aircraft somewhere he couldn't see and it made him miss his first home in the town, where the sounds of people would fill a warm day, whether garden radios or grass being cut, it was a sign of the holidays for people to withdraw from their box houses and spend time outside. In this house however the nearest neighbor was at least a mile away and the long drive and expanse of land on all sides ensured no encroachment of sight or sound in either direction.

This home, too, had been loved once. Bright hanging baskets that adorned the patio and fresh-cut flowers that filled the kitchen with sweet scent were looking listless by the time his parents returned from hospital with empty arms. From then they only continued a slow decay.

There had once been a novelty to the space of the farmhouse and the new land to explore, but he'd missed the proximity to his friends; that was until the steady deterioration of the house left him thankful for it.

He traipsed a path to the shed through the long, undisturbed grass. It was on the edge of the land, sat on a small strip of concrete next to the barren perimeter of the driveway. On approach it looked just as he remembered it, and thankfully far less ominous than it had from the upstairs window late last night. He'd not visited it since his Dad was around, when on a weekend they would bring broken and non-functioning bikes bought cheap and he would watch as his dad worked over them. In his own hands, tools felt clunky and uncoordinated like they were at odds with the mechanism of his hands. The instructions would muddy in his mind and he lacked patience. He was most content to just sit by and watch as his father stripped apart an engine or dismantled a section with such focus that his hands were fluid motion as they worked in the grime. But those memories were like looking into an old chest that you had but forgotten, he checked on them and then shut the lid, because there was a reason they'd been put aside and grown dust.

The lock was gone. Unstained wood and screw holes were where it once was. He glanced towards the house to make sure Dylan hadn't strayed. The door swung open with a gentle touch, and inside it was as he remembered. Shelves piled with tools and jars and old bottles of oil and lubricant that had discoloured with age.

He looked out towards the trees. The bright vista of summer foliage and clear sky made it hard to believe the events of last night had happened. But there had been marks on his skin when he'd dressed and the wall bore the carving of his temper.

He sent a message to Liana.

When he got in, his mother was getting ready to go. She had washed her hair and put on fresh clothes, but they did little to offset the gaunt appearance of her face. Hugh retreated to his room. Liana had replied to say she'd be there in twenty minutes. It was only at that point that Hugh considered he should probably have a last minute tidy up, but as quickly as the thought came, so did the counter thought that twenty minutes cleaning would barely begin a room, so he used the time instead to check on his brother. Dylan was downstairs playing on his games console. It left limited attention for conversation, so he ended up sitting and watching until Liana arrived.

They crossed the long grass to the woods. The drop in temperature and light from being under the full glare of the midday sun to within the shade of the trees was instant.

"Are we going back to the same place? You had me worried it was something urgent when you messaged me." Liana said.

"It is urgent. You'll see, hopefully."

The river appeared still like dark glass and dappled light spread across the barren dirt ground. The clearing held none of the threat that he had felt the night before. Liana stood by the water's edge. A dash of colour against the dark depths of the river caught her eye. It was a single, white waterlily in full bloom. She moved parallel to its position, marveling at the dainty petals that sat upon the wide, flat leaf as though levitating. Without touching them, she knew they would feel like velvet against her skin. The snow white morphed to a dusky pink where the petals joined, held around a yellow centre like sentinels to a crown.

She leaned in closer, surprised that such a flower was here. She was so focused on the flower she didn't notice the water breach the lily pads edges and begin creeping inwards towards the tips of the outermost petals. It only came to her attention when the flower began to drift towards her, now in direct contact with the water that formed a translucent layer atop the pads. It continued to travel towards the bank until it was only a foot away, close enough to perhaps reach if she were to stand right upon the edge of the bank where soft ground fell away and reach as far as she could. But at that point it stopped, the petals seeming to quiver in such a way that was near imperceptible.

She stepped closer, considering the potential danger of trying to grab it. She could feel the ground beneath her give slightly beneath her weight. She dropped to a crouch, not wishing to test the ground further. Now on a closer level to the lily, she felt sure it was within her reach. She stretched her hand out above the water's surface and brushed against one of the petals that, as they appeared, were like silk to touch. Another reach and she would take hold of it, but as her hand neared it, the lily bobbed away from her in a down and sideways movement, like a stringed balloon in the hands of an active child.

Hugh had not noticed Liana by the river. He was examining a note that he'd found by Gamel's self-fashioned log chair. He saw her leaning over the water on the bank in a precarious position.

"Get away from the water!" Liana shot back from the water

and got to her feet. "It's not safe."

"Have you found something?" she asked, noticing the paper in his hand.

He ignored her question and continued to study the note. He recognised the patterned edges of a sticky note pad that his mother kept in the kitchen. There was a short message written in a rough scrawl. It asked Hugh to meet with him to talk that night, so he could offer some explanation. Gamel's signature was at the bottom.

"I need to come back later," he said.

"What do you mean? You're not making sense."

"It's hard to explain. You remember when I told you about the horse?"

"Of course."

"Well, there's a man too," he said, lowering his voice. Liana's expression was wary.

"Are you in some kind of trouble?"

"No, it's ok, I think. But I want you to look at this horse."

"Sure, I want to help. You can use my computer too if you still need to."

"Thanks."

A low snorting noise came from the water. Sanna walked towards them, her coat wet and her pace steady; an entirely different creature from the one twelve hours before. Liana's eyes widened in surprise and she looked to Hugh.

"That's her. Don't get too close," he said.

Sanna stopped, keeping her distance. She turned her head to get a better look at Liana, her forelock draped over her eyes.

"She's beautiful." Liana said. "You're worried about her?"

"I just want to know if she seems normal to you, like other horses."

Liana reached out her hand and moved towards Sanna. Sanna's ears instantly pricked forwards in interest.

"Be careful."

"She's fine. I'm used to being around horses."

She held her palm by Sanna's muzzle. Sanna exhaled in blowing breaths as she took in her smell. Her neck was arched and she kept her head high. Liana studied the thick, dark mane that covered the horse's broad neck. It had been brushed and plaited in sections. She let out her breath, starting to relax. Sanna watched her with bright curiosity, her body still and tense. Her fingers traced against the wet texture of her shoulder, feeling it stick slightly to her skin.

"She has a strange coat, the texture is different," she said to Hugh, taking her eyes off Sanna.

Whilst they both locked eyes with each other, Sanna sprung into violent movement. Swinging her head round, she clasped the skin of Liana's upper arm between her teeth.

"Watch out!" Hugh said. Liana darted out of reach of Sanna, who was threatening to attack again, her ears pinned back flat.

"Are you ok?"

"No, that really hurt, what made her do that? She was ok a minute ago."

She was inspecting her arm, where a large purple mark now marked her skin. Now that the shock was wearing off, Hugh could see she was struggling with the pain.

"Stay behind me," he said.

Sanna stepped towards them and Hugh put himself between her and Liana. Sanna dipped her head and nudged his shoulder. When he put out his hand, she rested her head against the flat of his palm, her eyes soft and her ears forward.

Liana kept one hand over her bruised skin as she took a further look at Sanna. She dropped to a crouch, studying where white met grey below the horse's knee, and smooth coat turned into longer, coarser hair. The hoof caught her attention.

"There's something wrong with her hooves," she said,

wishing she could get closer to feel. "They're deformed or something."

He looked down at Sanna's hooves.

"What's wrong with them?"

"They look like they're backwards. I've never seen anything like it."

Sanna picked up the hoof they were studying and stamped it against the ground.

"We better get back, see if there's anything we can do for your arm," he said.

Liana nodded. She glanced at Sanna and met her cool stare. She felt discomfort breeding inside her as she met those unnerving black irises that possessed a calm assertiveness. It was not the demeanor usually seen in a flighty, prey animal. It was not equine.

"Please be careful tonight, are you sure it's safe?" she asked.

"Yeah. Gamel's my friend he wouldn't hurt me."

Liana looked sceptical.

"Have you considered telling your mum?"

"Like I'd tell her about anything."

They reached the house and Hugh stopped by the door.

"Just come round when you want to use my laptop. I'm free anytime."

"Sure, thanks."

He watched her walk away and then entered the house. Dylan and his mother were in the living room. Dylan was in his pyjamas ready for bed, but by the looks of it they had come down for some cartoons and the combination of a dimmed room, background noise and the weight of her son's body rested on her had sent their mother to sleep. Dylan didn't notice Hugh peering through the door, he was half asleep himself. He left them undisturbed.

When he woke, the hallway light was on but the house was silent. Dylan was asleep in his bed. He must have taken himself because downstairs the TV was still on, just a blue screen that threw the room in an eerie, blue illumination with the sleeping figure of his mother at its centre.

The track through the garden from the back door to the woods was now visible even in low light, only if you were to look directly down it though. If not, then the long grass surrounding it kept it hidden. The trail through the trees was likewise all too familiar by now, but the night always brought about that primitive alertness to his surroundings, so acute that it was impossible to relax.

When he got to the clearing, Sanna was dozing in the river, the water coming to her knees and her head lowered to just above the surface. A flick of an ear was the only sign that she saw him. He went straight to the fallen tree, placing the cooling bowl in its customary spot on the stump. Hugh knew better than to be fooled by his apparent solitude in the clearing. Gamel always bided his time. Sure enough, after a few minutes, Gamel stepped out of the trees and greeted Hugh with an affable grunt. Hugh waited while Gamel ate his porridge. He ate in huge mouthfuls of food, crouched over the bowl in the same manner of a person who does not see warm food often. He finished with a satisfied smack of the lips.

"So you saw what happened yesterday?" Hugh asked. There was a pause before Gamel replied.

"Yes."

"My brother could have been seriously hurt. He was terrified, what was wrong with her?"

Gamel sighed and the thick, misshapen fingers of his hands twitched.

"She has not been herself lately. The journey here took so much of her strength and moving has unsettled her. You would be wise to make sure your brother never comes near her again."

"He won't be. But what sort of horse attacks someone like that? That's not normal."

"She is not just a placid animal that you would find in any field. She is a proud creature who I know very well. She is not suited to living in this way, moving from one unsuitable place to another, and she is not tolerable of young, shrieking children."

"My brother didn't deserve that."

"I didn't say that he did." Gamel's stare was fixed on the ground. "Look, I know that yesterday was unpleasant, but Sanna needs protecting. This is all the more reason I need to find somewhere suitable for us to live, so that everyone is safe."

"You don't need to keep things from me. I'm your friend."

Gamel shifted in his seat, his new blanket draped across his aching knees. The shaky sound of his breathing betrayed his age.

"If I was to tell you about her, I'd be putting a great deal more trust in you than I'd give to anyone." Hugh nodded, waiting and listening. "Sanna is not simply a horse. You need to understand. She is as old as me, and I have always watched over her."

"Then what is she?"

"In our native country, she is folklore. She is possibly, now, the last of her kind." In the water, Sanna had perked up. She was watching them, entirely still. "What she did last night was part of her natural instinct. It didn't matter that it was your brother; she would have treated anybody the same."

"So she was trying to hurt him? To get him in the water?" Gamel looked uneasy. "What would have happened if she'd got him in the river?"

"I doubt if the water is deep enough here."

"And you said she's sick? Is there anything I can do to help?"

Gamel said nothing for a time. Sanna exited the water, sniffing at the ground before she lay down on the dirt and resumed her resting.

"She just needs to get her strength back," Gamel said. "The only thing that might help is raw meat. If you were able to get hold of that and bring it to me, it might do something."

"Ok, I'll try. There's something else."

"Yes?"

"Is there anything different about you?"

"What d'you mean by that?"

"I'm just wondering. You seemed to just disappear last night. You were there one minute then you were gone."

"I don't remember doing any such thing."

"I was standing right next to you."

"Pah." The sound was accompanied by a dismissive downwards pat of his hand, as if swatting a particularly incessant, bothersome insect. "Are you calling me a liar?"

"No, but-"

"The less you know about me the better." Hugh was quiet. He drew his hands into his pockets for warmth. "All I mean by that is there's nothing much for you to know, even less for you to be concerned about. How are things at home, anyway?"

"Mum had a good day, she made dinner," he said with a shrug. "My brother's just happy she's around for him to talk to but it never lasts long. If anything, a couple of days having her there just makes it harder on him when she's not."

"You don't think she'll change? Maybe she can get better?"

"Doubt it, unless something happened and made her then probably not. I give it two days tops and she'll be back to her usual self."

"She's not noticed your visits here then."

"No, she doesn't care about me." Hugh kicked the dirt with

the toe of his trainers. "You know, I wouldn't think any differently of you if there was something you wanted to tell me." He looked at Gamel from underneath his dark eyelashes. "We'd still be friends."

"I know, lad. It's for that reason that there's nothing I need to tell you. "

That settled the matter for Hugh, and as much as he didn't like it, he wouldn't press it. He stuffed his hands in his pockets and looked towards home.

"Well, I'm going to head back. I think one of my friend's dad is a butcher. I might be able to get meat through him."

"See you tomorrow."

Hugh took the empty bowl and spoon and made his way home, the night closing in on his tail like a crumbling bridge, quickening his step.

Chapter 9

The next morning, Hugh found both his mother and Dylan in the kitchen. His mother was still in her nightclothes, her long hair disarranged around her shoulders.

"Can we go somewhere? Mum? Please." Dylan said, dancing between them with an excess of energy.

"I don't know," Janet replied. "I need to wake up a bit first, I had next to no sleep last night."

"To the playground! Please mum, it's been ages."

"Well ok. Not for too long though." Hugh moved around her, trying to get something to eat without having to look at or speak to her. "Would you like to come along Hugh?"

He half heard her question, not taking much notice until Dylan chimed in with a multitude of pleases.

"What?" he replied, finishing a mouthful of food.

"I'm taking Dylan out somewhere, probably that local park he likes. Do you want to join us?" His mother rubbed her head where her headache still resided.

"Why would I want to do that?"

"Because you're part of this family too."

"Yeah well I don't want to play happy families today," he replied, heading for the door. His mother stopped him.

"Did you hear anything strange last night?"

"No, why?"

"I came down in the middle of the night. I'd been having an awful dream that woke me up. When I walked in here, all the pots and pans were on the side, and not long before that I thought I heard noises. Did you notice anything?"

"I probably left them out. As for the noises, maybe it's those pills you've started."

Hugh left the kitchen and his mother reached for the packet of antidepressants she'd been depleting. She pulled out the information sheet and began looking for the side effects.

When his mother and Dylan had left, Hugh slipped out of the house. Despite Liana's insistence that he needn't give notice, he messaged her to say he would come round. She was waiting by the door.

"My parents are out again so don't worry about them," she said, sitting at the desk in her bedroom where her laptop was on. She had set out another chair for Hugh.

"I want to look at Google Maps," he said. She let him take over, watching as he located his house.

"Are you looking for something?"

"Yeah, I need to find a place not too far, with water and some kind of building or shelter. See if you can see anything."

He began to search outwards from the general area of the woods, squinting his eyes to scan closely every landmark and natural feature he could make out. Liana leant in close. He could hear her breathing by his cheek.

"I take it this is to do with that man, the one that owns the horse," she said.

"If I tell you, you need to keep it a secret." She looked at him and nodded.

"Of course."

"I'm trying to help him find somewhere to live permanently. He says any kind of shed or outbuilding would be fine."

"Are you sure that's the right thing to do? Maybe there're other options-"

"No. I talked to him about it already. I told him I'd look."

They found nothing in the immediate area of the woodland or around the housing estate at its rear. Hugh scrolled further.

"Stop," Liana said. Hugh zoomed in on the body of water that grew to fill the screen. "Look on the bottom right edge. I saw something there."

"You know this place?"

"It's the country park. I've been there a few times." She moved her hand to the laptop pad and directed the view. Within minutes she had found the small brown shape that looked to be some kind of building. "It's well away from the paths and right by the water."

"It looks great," Hugh said. "Could we print it? Get the directions?"

"Sure. You want to do it right now?" he thought for a moment. "If you leave it with me, I can draw the route."

"Ok, yeah. Thanks.

He left Liana's, pleased with what they'd found. But rather than turn left towards home, he cut right and went to Ben's. After a short wait on the narrow porch, Ben opened the door, breathless and with flushed cheeks.

"Hugh, how's it going?"

"You got my message, yeah? Is it ready?"

"Yeah, I'll go get it for you, got a bag of it. My dad didn't even ask questions, just said there's plenty." Ben turned and began lumbering out of sight. He paused at a doorway to shout out to Hugh. "Come in if you like, Kain's here."

"I'll wait, thanks."

After a few minutes, Ben reappeared with a blue plastic bag that looked heavy with its contents. Before Hugh could take it, Kain appeared at Ben's shoulder.

"What's that you've got?" he asked. Ben looked between the two of them.

"Nothing important," Hugh said.

"Let me see?" Kain pushed forwards and tried to look into the bag, but he moved back. "Is this how it is now? You're keeping secrets?" Kain switched his gaze to Ben.

"It doesn't concern you," Hugh said.

"So it is like that. We're not friends now?"

"A friend wouldn't have said what you said the other night." He looked at Ben. "Thanks, mate." He gave a nod and turned to leave.

"Guess you can't take a joke when it's aimed at you. You know you really need to lighten up." Kain was out the doorway now, a half-rolled cigarette unravelling in his fingers. "I can find out if I wanted to!" he shouted, but Hugh was beyond listening.

The days began to pass in what was becoming a routine. The cupboards were stocked and there was porridge for Gamel. He took the meat on that first night, leaving it as an offering before slipping back home by himself. It was a few days later, as he and Gamel sat by a well-stoked fire watching the calm pass of water nearby that he felt a surge of affection and attachment for the old man he'd come to know. The moon had come full circle overhead as under the trees Hugh sat sipping from the thermos that they now shared.

"I know that you're in a bad situation, and I really hope you find somewhere to stay soon. But all the same, I'm glad that I met you and you're still here."

Gamel took a turn of the flask and sipped its steaming contents.

"Do you mean that?"

"Yes," he replied, with no hint of doubt in his voice. "It means a lot to me having someone to talk to. Sometimes when I'm at home all the time, I just feel so trapped. I feel like there's no one who understands me. Even though I have friends, they're so wrapped up in their own dramas; It just makes me feel like I'm different sometimes, like I don't belong. And when I try to make an effort, and try to put it to the back of my mind and be social, it's like my body works against me. Everything locks up and I get so hung up on doing the right thing, saying the right thing, that I end up doing nothing at all. It beats me. So that's why I find it easier sometimes to just be alone and stop trying, but since I met you and we've been talking, it's given me something to look forward to. I guess just someone to speak to without having to worry about everything. Do you know what I mean?"

"Yes lad, I do," Gamel replied with a voice like gravel.

"And with the help you've been giving in the house, that's made a big difference, too. It even seems like my mum might be starting to change for the better."

"I'm glad to hear it. I would guess that the reason you're having a hard time is because you have a lot more to worry about than your friends. They don't have to think about looking after their little brother or making dinner like you do."

Hugh dropped his head and twisted his hands in his lap.

"I know the easiest thing to do is to avoid it and shut yourself up away from everyone," Gamel continued. "It might feel like that's what you want to do, but as I'm sure you know, it doesn't make you feel good. And it won't, because it doesn't make anyone feel good to push everyone away, not in the long term."

Hugh thought over Gamel's words. "Well I have you, and I trust you. I have another friend I speak to when she's around, but I don't think I'll ever be close with my mum."

Gamel watched the flames as they licked at the night air. Hugh thought his mind was somewhere else, not totally here in the clearing.

"If anyone should know about loneliness lad, it's me. I've spent more years than I care to consider living on my own, avoiding people. But that's the life I've been dealt, and experience has taught me to accept it. Now I don't know that I ever had a family, if I did they're long gone, but from my understanding you got a family of your own back in that house. It may be small, and one may be young for now and the other not too well for the time being but they're there all the same. Don't forget it."

"Dylan means everything to me, he always will. The only thing me and my mum have in common is we live under the same roof."

"Well, just remember that even though you might not feel close to them now, you've got plenty of people that care. I could go missing tomorrow and you'd be the only person to even notice. However intelligent Sanna is I doubt she would do more than turn her head if I was to cease to exist," Gamel said, a smile pulling on the corners of his mouth.

"I would care."

"What?" Gamel didn't catch his drift.

"I'd care if you disappeared. I don't want you to."

Gamel made a huffing noise that sounded appreciative but didn't stretch to a thank you. Sanna appeared to be sleeping. Lying down in the clearing with her braided mane trailed in the dirt.

"Has the meat helped?" he asked Gamel.

"Yes lad, thank you."

"I can get more, however much you need. I had a look on the map as well, the one on the computer."

"Did you see anything?"

Hugh paused for a moment, watching Sanna's sides move with her steady respiration and the calm conscience of her depthless eyes.

"Not yet. I'll have to keep looking."

All the talk of his family and his mother weighed heavily on Hugh's mind as he got through the following day. He had assumed it would be another day that they would go without passing more than small talk, but realised he was wrong when after coming down for a snack he found his mother waiting for him in the kitchen. Not a good sign. She stood next to an open drawer, its contents half strewn on the counter and some spilling on the floor. For some incomprehensible reason she was wielding her phone in one hand; the way she held it and the fierce stare of her eyes told him he was about to spend ten minutes learning why.

"I found this in the paper drawer. Do you realize what this is?"

"It's your phone." Hugh couldn't stop the slip of sarcasm.

"Well, can you tell me why I found this, along with Dylan's mp3 player, in the bread bin? Along with one half of the scales, the radio, and the-" she paused, distracted by the sight of a handle protruding from the open drawer's contents. "-the handheld whisk? Is this some sort of wind-up?"

Hugh now saw how the objects were crammed in. He could guess who was responsible.

"I-." he began.

"I'm sick of this. You just have no regard for any of my stuff you just move it around or shove it in a drawer." His mother gave the disheveled drawer a hefty shove, the radio hitting the fitting with a bang before rebounding with force and sending more papers flying to the floor. She paced, muttering to herself and leaving Hugh to stand and wait, relieved there was now no need to claim insanity.

"I know you're trying to help Hugh, and I really appreciate your effort, but you can't treat important things like that."

She stalked out of the room, falling into the same chair she would fail to move from for the rest of the day.

Hugh prepared his food in an irritable silence, shifting around the table not wishing to sit. His eyes moved over what littered its surface, some plates, the day's letters and a newspaper his mother had brought back from the shop. He turned it over with one hand, looking to distract his thoughts, scanning over the headlines. What he saw made him stop his chewing. He took the paper to the living room, bursting in on his mother in a way that made her grip her chair and open her eyes wide.

"What is it?"

"Have you read this?"

She took it from him with pale, shaking fingers and read it her usual slow way, reading and re-reading the small print.

"They're searching for a man, he was last seen going into Scythe woods, he could be out there right now."

"They found his dog?" Her brow creased, her comprehension struggling to come up to speed.

"Yeah, they found it by the road but the man wasn't with him."

"Joseph Argoyle-" she said, drawing out the name. "We don't know this man, why are you so worried about it?"

"He could be right out there." He gestured to the trees beyond the walls.

"They'll find him, if he's alive. They'll do a proper search."

Hugh drew back into the doorway.

"Hugh?" she said, her eyes staring out from where she sat in the dim space. "I don't want you going out there. It might not be safe."

"Why would I go out there?"

"I know you used to spend a lot of time with your dad out there; It must hold a lot of memories."

Hugh felt his chest blaze with sudden heat and his hands turn to tight fists.

"I don't care about my dad," he said, turning away from the room and beginning to breathe hard. "You know nothing."

Upstairs he shut himself in his room with a slam of the door.

He would wait now, wait until he'd settled and could slip out of the house without drawing attention to himself.

Downstairs, his mother gave in to the hold of the black shroud she tenanted inside her mind.

"Gamel?" Hugh moved through the trees that bordered the clearing, trying to make out any figures in the dark. "I need to speak to you about something. It's important."

His steps began to slow when he realised that Gamel wouldn't come. He started to feel the cold in his fingers and the dampness in the air. Home seemed like a long way away. The branches reached and grabbed like claws and the ground appeared like a writhing black carpet that wished to consume his trainers.

He heard a low whickering noise, something friendly. Sanna was in the water facing him. He was glad to move out of the trees. He approached the bank and kept eye contact with Sanna, her eyes were soft and inviting and her ears pricked forwards towards him in eager waiting. He stopped short of the water, careful to keep his feet on dry land.

"Come here, girl," he said, stretching out his palm. She was unwilling to move. At first she stood, calm and immobile. Then, with a shake of her head, she walked forwards, coming out of the water to meet him.

He rubbed her all over. The first tentative touches over her neck and shoulder became sweeping strokes over her back and the hard muscle of her haunches. Hugh began to relax. He could sense that she trusted him, and despite his cautious fear, the readiness to jump back if she made any sudden movement, he at once felt a wash of happiness. He marveled in the pure white of her coat, the smooth lines of her strong legs.

She turned her head and nudged his legs, pushing upwards. Hugh could sense what she wanted, but remembered the first time he'd been on her back, the ground falling away from him and having no control. He stepped away but still she persisted, tossing her head and moving her shoulder towards him. He let his hands rest on her back, watching for any signs of the aggression he'd witnessed before. Under his touch, Sanna lay down with a gentle thud onto the dirt. He crouched beside her and spoke at little more than a murmur.

"Don't hurt me," he breathed, leaning forward and putting some of his weight onto her back. "If I trust you, don't take me to the water."

He leant over her slowly, ready to spring away at any explosive reaction from the horse. But she showed no sign of agitation. He took a breath and raised one leg over her, taking a tight grasp of the closest section of mane. Sanna seemed to wait for him to settle, then stood up in one fluid movement, Hugh hunching forwards as he tried not to become unbalanced.

Rather than hurtle towards the water as he feared she would, Sanna seemed unperturbed by his being on her back. She sniffed the ground, scattering the loose leaves. Hugh sat upright, his hands entwined in the coarse length of her hair. He was dizzy with exhilaration. The sight and feel of the horse beneath him was overwhelming. That she trusted him to ride her and to share in her strength and power. He tried to relax his bunched muscles and get his position secure.

Sanna turned to face the water and raised her head, her ears flicking forwards to where she looked.

"Steady," Hugh said to her, gripping her sides with his knees. "Just stay here." One white ear swiveled round towards his voice, but her entire focus seemed to remain on the river. She tightened beneath him, her body like a wound coil. She took a tentative step, the movement like a release. Quicker steps followed, and she broke into a trot. The sudden jerky motion made Hugh hunch forward and hold on to her best he could. He didn't feel slippy though, his legs seemed to stick around her sides and his hands against her neck found an easy hold on her coat.

He heard the splash of the water as they entered the river and she slowed against the drag of the current. His reaction was automatic. He pushed away from her with a swing of his outer leg, landing on his feet as he used her for support. Cold water swallowed his feet and lower legs and he went pale at the chill. He stumbled backwards, dragging his feet across the stony riverbed. Sanna tossed her head and made a move towards him. She pushed him over, her head barging into his chest. Hugh scrambled backwards, seeing only a blur of white moving above him.

He stood on the bank, shaking with wet and cold. Sanna was eyeing him without concern.

"Thanks for that," he said. She made no response. He returned home to get changed and dry.

Chapter 10

The weekend approached and Hugh hadn't seen Gamel for days. Only the empty bowl and spoon each day showed he was still there. There was a change in his mother. After asking him about strange noises in the night, she seemed to have become wary of dusk's daily approach. Rather than settle sleepily to rest or retire to her room, she had taken to perching in her armchair or at the kitchen table, staring at her laptop or a battered book with eyes that were slightly too alert. She gave away her anxiety by the way that she chewed her nails absently or made paces round the kitchen, checking the door and watching out of the window. He had not once seen her go to bed at night. If she crashed for a doze, she would wake with a start, make coffee, and resume her sitting activity. Even when he stayed up until the early hours, she was still downstairs. Yet when he woke late morning, she would be tucked away in bed, her body catching a reprieve. He hadn't expected her somewhat of a normal mother routine to last, although she was still taking the medication, often left out of its packet on the side. With her regression to retreating to bed by day, he had been back to watching Dylan. He still enjoyed playing out back. The only difference now was that he kept a careful distance away from the woodland's edge.

The day had that drawn out quality of long and lazy summer days, when the heat sapped the energy from your body. Both boys had gone inside to escape the heat, and Hugh put on a film. His phone alert sounded from his pocket; it was Liana asking how he was.

"Are you going to be ok to stay here and watch this film if I go to see a friend?"

"When will you be back?" Dylan asked.

"Before it's finished. You just stay here, don't leave the house."

Liana perched on the end of her bed. The light from the window made her look pale and drawn.

"Have you heard about this?" she held out her phone.

"What is it?"

"The man that was missing, they've found his body."

"Let me see." She passed him the phone and he squinted at the screen. It was a news article. Beneath the headline was a photo of a man in his seventies, alive and happy. By its side, an aerial picture of the woods; Hugh could see the edge of his garden on the very left side. "He was in there then."

"In the river, the industrial end." Liana's expression was sincere. Hugh returned her phone. "Kain's been asking questions, you know. About me and you, what we're doing."

"How does he know we've been seeing each other?"

"I just mentioned it. I didn't realise you'd fallen out."

Hugh shrugged and turned away.

"I'm not worried about Kain. And I'm not worried about the body either."

Liana dropped her gaze.

"There was another reason I wanted to see you, the main one anyway. That place we found, I thought it'd be good if we can get a look at it, see if it's ok. I told my mum that I need to go to the country park for a summer homework assignment, she wants to go there anyway so we're going this afternoon."

"Right." Hugh nodded, frowning.

"There's space in the car, d'you want to come with us?"

"I told Dylan I wouldn't be too long."

"Oh, ok."

"I want to. It'd be best if I could see it for myself. I'll see if my mum can watch Dylan for a bit, then I can come."

"Ok, hope you can."

He got home and returned to an empty living room, the film still running. He called out for Dylan, but had no response. All the upstairs rooms other than his mothers were empty. He pushed through the back door into the garden, panic rising in his chest like a balloon.

"Dylan?" he called. He took a deep breath. "Dylan!"

"Over here." Dylan said, his voice faint and far away.

"Come in now, Dylan. I need to speak to mum about something."

He heard the tinkly sound of child's laughter floating across the thick, humid air.

"Can you see me?" Dylan said. Only long shoots of grass and weeds scattered with upturned old garden toys faced him. He heard a low giggle and pinpointed the sound to an area that had not been on his radar. It came from the old wooden play frame to the east. Disused, it stood alarmingly close to the tree line. With close inspection he thought he could just make out a strip of blue clothing. Dylan's face emerged from behind one of the thick wooden pillars with a grin that stretched its full width.

"Come on!" Hugh shouted, and his brother ran to join him.

They went inside and Hugh made a beeline for his mother's bedroom. He opened the door and let it hit the wardrobe with a belated thud, like a second herald of his appearance.

"Mum, wake up," he said, but today he had no patience for waiting. "Wake up!"

He pulled the duvet off her face and shoulder.

His mother made a noise that sounded like words half formed and groped with her hand for the cover.

"Wake up. I'm going out, you need to look after Dylan."

His voice broke slightly. His shoulders began to heave in

time with his breathing as he stood and watched for movement. When there was none he took the cover with both hands this time and flung it on the floor. His mother curled her knees towards her stomach, her nightdress riding up in a manner that was most unflattering. Her face crumpled inwards like a kicked can. Her lips pushed out like a petulant child.

"I can't Hugh, I can't I'm sorry." she drawled as if drunk. One of her hands came to rest on her forehead as if blighted by a great pain there. Hugh looked about himself. The walls felt close, trapping him in every direction, every side, floor to ceiling. He drew in a deep breath.

"Get up!" he roared. It was a sound as deep as it was loud. A tinge of guilt hit him for his younger brother who surely heard, but that came and went. The focus of his anger was a still stationary figure whose only reaction was to tighten the close of her eyes, like a child forever wishing on a birthday candle.

He stooped to the floor and scooped up a paperback that lay there. Still bent, he flung it with one hand towards the opposite wall with all his strength; propelled by rage. The book hit the wall with an abrupt smack sound and then dropped to the floor, splaying its pages. His mother drew up her other hand to cover her eyes and her body jolted at every bang as Hugh threw more items against the wall. A hairbrush hit the wall with such force that it bounced off, hitting the bedside table on its rapid descent to the floor and almost dislodging an old cup of tea. His mother began to sob in dry heaves that shook her entire frame. He looked upon her with a pity sourced from disgust. There was nothing he could do.

He replied to tell Liana that he couldn't join her, but he'd like her to call him and report back on how suitable it was. He spent the next two hours watching a film with Dylan, only watching in the physical sense of looking at the screen, his mind was far away. On a trip to the bathroom, he noted through the open door that his mother was once again covered with her duvet. She must have got up off the bed to retrieve it. The thought revived a dull hatred.

When evening drew in, both boy's thoughts turned to food. Hugh had forgotten about lunch, so they had picked on whatever was available throughout the day. Now hunger had set in. Their mother appeared at six o'clock. She checked in on them, tablets and a glass of water in hand, but did little more than mumble. Dylan asked if she was making dinner and she replied that she was. Soon the smell of cooking food reached them and their mother called for them to come to the kitchen. Hugh shuffled in behind Dylan, who bounded to the table at top speed and sat at the small space that was clear. Hugh stood with his back to the wall, having no desire to be in the company of his mother but feeling drawn to the food in a way he could not resist.

Their mother was bustling round the kitchen in an aggravated state, muttering to herself a constant despair at the lack of utensils and clean plates. She flustered from one side of the kitchen to the other, her frustration growing as she complained to the empty space that nothing was where it should be. She resigned herself to having to hand wash three plates and some cutlery from the stack in the sink. They rather sensibly kept their mouths shut as they watched and waited.

Soon she picked up the gloves and pulled open the oven door, filling the room with the smell of hot, baking cheese. Hugh's mouth watered as she pulled out the plastic tray, which appeared to be a family size, ready prepared macaroni cheese.

Their mother had not calmed down. She spun on her heels to take it to the plates, irritation at the boy's inactivity rather than offering to help gnawing on her as it grew. She went to set the tray down but realised she had no spoon to serve it with, so turned again, shifting the tray to the palm of her left hand and freeing her right to open the utensil draw. She selected a serving spoon, but in her haste started to turn back before closing the drawer. As she tried to shut it behind her, her focus shifted away from the balancing tray. It slid from her hand like a well-greased fish.

It took everyone by surprise. Even watching it leave beyond gravity's tender hold and then free-fall through four short feet of air, it did not register in Hugh's mind that his dinner was in jeopardy until the floor hit. The tray of hot pasta and cheese connected with the ground in a wet splat sound, spilling its contents in a spreading heap. No-one spoke. Hugh watched, their mother blinked and Dylan stared at his mother's face, too short to see what had become of their dinner but knowing that the food was no longer in his mother's hands and her face had set all wrong. Their mother broke the pause, whipping the gloves off her hand with startling speed and throwing them to the ground. She looked to be on the verge of speaking, but her lips pursed and did no more, proceeding only to storm out of the kitchen to the sound of her slipper clad feet slapping against the linoleum and the catch of sobs deep in her throat.

Both boys watched this still without moving or speaking. They heard her bedroom door shut with a slam. Hugh's stomach ached with emptiness, the scent of baked food now well and truly filled the kitchen. He shifted forwards from the wall and approached the cheese-laden floor. Following his lead, Dylan hopped off his chair and looked around the counter top that had been blocking his view. The way in which he peered around it suggested that he knew it wasn't good news, but that didn't stop him bursting into wet tears when he saw the fate of his long awaited dinner.

"Stop crying, Dylan," Hugh said. His brother cried louder, more insistently.

"Stop crying," he repeated, his brother quietened slightly.

Hugh swallowed hard. He reached out and touched the upturned tray; it had already cooled. He took a careful hold of either end and righted it while trying to scoop the remaining pasta. Most flowed out as he tipped it and added to the considerable macaroni puddle, but he kept a small amount that the floor had not spoilt. He put it onto Dylan's plate under his watchful, teary gaze. His crying turned to abject sniffs that began to grow further apart now that he was back at the table with a plate of warm food.

Hugh returned to the mess and picked up one of the newly washed forks. Crouching behind the counter, he used another plat□e to scoop more for himself, but it had spread into a thin layer. He ate, still crouched. Despite its landing on a floor that had not seen a mop for months, the macaroni hit his empty stomach with warm delight. He only meant to eat a small amount, enough to satiate his hunger, but he had an entire plateful before he stopped. Dylan got down from the table.

"Is there any more?" he asked.

"No, I need to clean this up." Hugh replied, looking at the now even further spread mess. He cleared it up with a kitchen towel.

He checked his phone. There was still no reply from Liana. Faced with the monotony of the same cartoons and the continued lack of his mother, he felt desolate and alone. The early evening sun cast a warm and inviting light outside. He needed a change of scene. He checked the clock; It was early, but he got Dylan ready for bed. They looked over the pictures of his favourite story book until the pages ended and it was time for Hugh to go.

"Are you going somewhere?"

"Stay in your bed. Don't leave the house."

"But Hugh-"

"I'll be back by the morning. Mum's only down the hall."

"She won't get up-"

"I'm going." Hugh said, smoothing down the duvet. "Go to sleep."

By the back door, he shrugged on a light jacket and stepped outside. He had checked over the map again and knew he only needed to stick to the river heading northwards from the house and he should reach the body of water shown as a blue blip on the paper.

He crossed the expanse of lawn without a single look back. Whereas his usual gait was loping and casual, now he made great purposeful strides across the grass. Rather than taking the right to go to the clearing, he continued ahead until the path reached its end. Without pause he carried on, still tracking north with the river to his right. The trees were thick here, and the ground proved difficult to navigate as it was potholed with rabbit runs and nettle sprawls. The crack of breaking sticks came with every step.

The trees grew sparse and he saw the bridge that connected the footpath from his end of the village with the housing estate where Kain and Ben lived. Head down, he passed it hoping nobody was watching. He was back amongst a gathering of birch trees and the soft tread of a woodland floor, although the proximity to houses saw it littered with cans and crisp packets.

He reached the perimeter fence that marked the outer edge of the town. Ducking under the top rail he was free of the trees. Space stretched out before him in the form of a large crop field. He'd come out at a corner where the river to the right of him continued straight along its edge, bordered by bushes and an even steeper bank.

It was a struggle to keep his trainers from sinking into the dense, ploughed ground, but he walked along its edge until he came to a solid hedgerow blocking his path. There was only a slim gap where the hedgerow ended at the banks precipice. He was sure he could inch around it, but on the other side it joined with a barbed wire fence to contain the sheep grazing beyond. He tried to get a grip on a branch or anything he could hold as he tried to get to the other side, impeded by the steep drop to the water. The hedge gave him nothing to grasp, only thin twigs that although strong, bit into his hand when he applied pressure. He could tell that putting his weight onto one would cut into his hand if it didn't give and drop him to the river. He had no choice but to give up his effort to remain clean and get to the ground. He used his hands to hold his body upright as his feet cautiously dropped over the edge of the ground and got a toehold in the rutted dirt. In this way he sidled around the hedge and find a small patch of ground the other side, just big enough to stand on whilst he appraised the wire fence that now blocked him. After a few seconds of consideration he took off his jacket and placed it over the wire snag teeth that lay in wait, some with macabre trophies of sheep's wool impaled on their rusty barbs.

He tried his weight on the fence, although softened by the jacket, it was still sharp. He pushed it down low enough to swing his leg over, then with one quick movement he jumped up and shifted his weight sharply forwards to escape the painful catch in his crotch, ending up doing a comical dive as he drew his other leg up and over behind him. .

Things were easier after that. He continued to walk through field after field either climbing over gates and fences or getting through or around hedgerows. The river stayed to his side, ebbing and flowing through overgrown, murky wells and occasionally opening out to a wide channel where the surface was undisturbed. When he'd set out, evening had been just starting to draw in. Now the light had all but faded and the air had changed. It seemed thinner, quicker. It rushed around him in unsettling gusts in the dark.

He was in a crop field, miles from home. Progress had been slow. He thought from the line of trees ahead and the distant chimney tops that he was approaching a road, although it wasn't one he recognised. He walked on and as he suspected soon came across the huge tracks of a tractor that led to an open gate. The river fell away to the mouth of a bridge and he found himself on a quiet country road that approached him coming down a shaded hill before running over the bridge and curving away up another gentle slope towards small rows of quaint houses.

He heard the low rumble of an approaching engine. It would pick him up as a strange figure in a ripped jacket standing as though dazed by the side of the road, so he ducked through a gap in the fence by the bank and hid behind a nearby tree. The sound of the car grew louder and its bright headlights scoped the road as it passed by and ascended the hill away from him. Hugh wondered why he'd felt the need to hide. Was it because of the guilt that coloured his thoughts of home? Or because for any normal teenager, disappearing with no notice on a summer's evening and not returning by nightfall evening would prompt worried calls. His mother probably had no idea he'd left. In fact, if he was to not return he supposed it wouldn't be until tomorrow afternoon that she'd even realise he'd gone. Unless Dylan alerted her, having woken up in the morning or after a nightmare in the night and realising that his brother was not there as promised. He looked towards home. Despite the dark he was sure he would get back. But he'd come too far to turn back now.

On the other side of the road, a considerable metal gate and wall blocked his path. He heard more cars so retreated to the bank, but rather than wait, he descended the slope to the water. In the gloom, the water looked black, but he knew it was shallow by the soft babbling it produced and the dim ripples on the surface. He peered under the bridge where it was wide and cavernous and removed his shoes and socks, holding them in one hand. He dipped a cautious toe in the water. The chill went straight to his core, but once his foot was submerged he began to adapt to it like the cool embrace of an ice pack. The day had been hot enough that it was not unpleasant. The stones were rough and the riverbed was silty against his toes.

He took quick steps, trying to reduce the time his feet bore weight upon them for fear of sinking into the river. Within the tunnel of the bridge the sound of water echoed around him like an ethereal chorus and the walls bore down all around him in a screen of black and green from the wet moss that leeched on their wet bricks.

He had a sudden fear that leeches lay in ambush of his white pale feet. That they prepared to feast on his blood and that he would raise his foot in a shock of pain and disgust to find it now black and convulsing with preying creatures. He rushed towards the open, finding that the flat, rocky bed only remained for another few feet before it plunged as a miniature waterfall and continued the river's natural course.

He waded to the right-side bank, climbing onto the grass and drying his feet with his jacket before replacing his socks and shoes. They were not perfectly dry and the chill of the water would take a while to subside, but the discomfort didn't bother him. He squeezed under the top wire rail of another sheep field and carried on walking. Under the gaze of many distrustful, grazing sheep he followed the river until he came to the border of the next field, an old footbridge crossing the river to his left.

An inquisitive horse that had been resting near the gate watched with interest as a disheveled and weary footed teenage boy clambered over the fence into his field. Hugh stopped to say hello, picking up a clasp of grass in offering. The horse took it gently from his hands with velvety lips, staring at Hugh with deep brown, placid eyes. Hugh stroked his nose, and he realised how different this horse was to Sanna, who acted with a permanent air of guarded integrity. Seeing that he had nothing else edible to offer, the horse returned to his content grazing.

Hugh tracked to the edge of the river again. Dense weeds had grown so long that they covered the surface almost completely from sight, bowed over with their own weight, and leaning across the water. It was impossible to tell how deep it was. His eye was caught by what looked like a large pond just beyond the far bank. He turned and jogged back to the footbridge he'd just passed. On its other side, a chained gate blocked his way. Paying no heed to the sign warning off trespassers, he clambered over it, feeling it snag against his jeans.

He was in a shaded walkway that ran through a copse of tall trees. They met above his head to form a dark tunnel that fed his unease. Night had fallen now like a cloak drawn over the sky, and a hidden insulation of clouds hid all stars from view. He walked down the path that led beneath the high branches, his breath escaping him in muted bursts. It opened out to a grassy area which forked towards a large, distant house up a long hill on the left where the grass tracks led; on the right was the body of water he'd been seeking.

He approached the water, testing the ground to see that his footing was safe. He stopped near the edge. He thought the area would be more than suitable for what Gamel was looking for; It looked deep and was of a good size. He tried to make out any kind of outbuilding or structure, but could see none from his vantage point. At the far end, the land was well hidden by a spread of wide trees and tangled weeds and grass that were as high as his middle.

The ground became uneven and he had to raise his arms for balance. His feet were nothing but murky shapes beneath him. A strange noise in the grass ahead startled him; maybe his mind was playing tricks. As he went to take another step, there was no ground to meet him. There was a sickening lurch in his stomach as he fell through the lush plants and landed with not firm ground but an icy wet that swallowed him with startling greed. He let out an involuntary gasp of shock and found himself up to his knees in water that was so thick with growth it was like sludge. The feeling of it crawling against his skin was repulsive. It was one of the leading waterways to the small lake, narrow and hidden by the overgrown greenery that thrived here.

He reached for the dry land in front of him, but a throng of nettles grown to an unnatural size had taken residence there, and covered his fingers with painful stings. He began to shake in reaction to the cold. The closest clear part of the bank he could see was a few meters away where the channel opened out. He figured this was his best option. He waded towards the deeper water, keeping close to the bank. It rose to his diaphragm but he could just about keep his feet grounded. The image of the leeches fixed to his skin flashed through his mind, and he was thankful for the cover of his trainers despite the absorbent weight of them combined with his clothes. He dragged his heavy legs through the water, his chest bobbing as if it were a weighted float with every draw of night air to his overworked lungs. He was close now. The clear bank was almost within touching distance.

Something long and sinewy brushed against his leg. It had thin strands that trailed against and around him like dead man's fingers. His panic grew and he dropped a hand into the water to brush away the likely weed, but looking down was a mistake for all he saw was a terrifying abyss of black glass. It looked like he had lost his lower half within a deep pool of sinister onyx. Not even his own reflection accompanied him.

He raised his head, vowing not to look down again. His breathing was stalling with the exposure to wet and cold. The water seemed to press down and around his chest, his airways seemed to tighten. He was only two steps away from salvation. He forced his leg forward; it felt separate from his body. It should have brought him within reaching distance of the bank, but the riverbed seemed to drop away to nothing and the water rushed towards his face. He tried to kick his feet, flay with his arms for some upward motion but his body had begun to seize and his muscles were shutting down.

Some faraway part of his mind was screaming at him. It said he was in danger. That he would drown out here in the dark and the cold with no-one to help. It was background noise, some distant information that came secondary to what was now floating on the water a short distance away. Perfect white, a single Lilly was resting on the calm surface beyond where he was struggling.

He went down again. This time painfully aware of the danger he was in. He fought with all he had, trying to force life back into his cold locked limbs. The water closed over him and tried to push into him. His legs finally came to life, pushing him above the surface and allowing him to take in some air with great gasps. He knew he didn't have long. He'd taken in some of the acrid water when he'd been under and it burnt in his airway, making him cough whilst he struggled.

Though his vision was blurry, he saw Sanna where the water was shallow. Her coat seemed to glow with the reflection of the finger width moon and her mane hung about her lowered head like the wispy shawl of a wraith, taken with the breeze.

"Sanna," he said with a weak gasp. It hurt his chest to speak. One white ear flicked in his direction and there was no escaping the cold now. There was no escaping the water. His legs ceased to move and as he began to sink, he saw her move towards him like a white vision. He reached to her with the last energy in his cramped, bloodless hands. He couldn't see, couldn't breathe, but he found the smooth hump of her shoulder come beneath him and he let himself sink onto her. He tried to recover his breathing, his arms locked around her neck as his chest came to rest across the slope of her back. Though he could hardly see, he sensed they were moving. Her skin was so cold, far colder than any living thing he'd touched before.

There was a sensation of rising, of being lifted from the water. The ground hit him hard as he slipped from her and landed on the bank. He had nothing left. His sight was an indistinct darkness and where he wasn't numb, his body hurt. He was slipping away, consciousness like an unattainable memory. There was something grabbing at him, a death grip of hands that captured him, strong as any he knew. The dead man's hands.

Chapter 11

Hugh woke in his bed to the sight of familiar walls. His first sensation was pain. His head seemed to swell with an awful pulsating headache that put to rest any ideas of getting back to sleep. He realised why his bed felt so strange; his pillow was beneath his legs to raise them, and he was lying on a towel. He pushed the duvet away and strained his neck to look at his body. He was stripped down to his underwear, his wet clothes folded on the floor. He tested his legs, seeing if he could swing at least one out of bed, but rather than swing, his leg dragged across the surface of the towel and awoke the dreadful ache that now permeated through his every fibre. He sat up with the grace of a man who has woken from anesthetic and is waiting for the pain. It was there all right. He could feel it as numbness in his extremities and a hammer in his core. His head felt stuffed up with a bad cold and his throat as if lined with razor wire.

There was a note on his bedside table. It was written in the familiar scrawl of someone who even now after having written many notes, still did not seem to be able to gauge the correct pressure to apply on a pencil. As a result the writing was punctuated with black etches and lead dust from where the tip had reached breaking point. It read:

Stay warm. Drink Fluids. Eat.

Hugh looked at the note for a while, not really seeing it. He tried to cast his thoughts back to last night. He remembered the feel of the hands, taking hold of him as he lay helpless on the bank. He thought he could remember looking up at the slice of ice moon whilst those same rough hands worked over his body on a bed of grass, and the rocking movement of being carried came to him with such assimilation that he had to grip the edge of his mattress to quell the nausea it provoked.

He put away those troubling thoughts for later, feeling a desperate need to wet his mouth and throat. He tried to call for Dylan, but only managed a hoarse spitting sound that died in his mouth. He stood on shaky legs and opened his door onto the quiet hall. It struck him as strange that after the night he'd had, the house and its occupants were as they always were; mundane, inactive, nothing was different. He could not expect the care of an attendant however ill he was.

Downstairs his mother was in the kitchen, her back to the door. She startled when he turned the tap on next to her to pour a glass of water. Turning away, he concentrated on getting through every painful swallow. A hollow bang came from the counter behind him. His mother had knocked over a clay pot. It was her turn to keep her back to him and act as though he wasn't there. Her hands patted the air over the cluttered counter, as if sorting or binding them with a force he could not see. They went to her sides, as if drying her hands as she rubbed the hip of her jeans, and then resumed their pandering to and sorting of the countertop. It occupied little of his attention, his foggy thoughts turning to resting.

"Were you out last night?" she asked him.

"What do you care?" he replied in a croaky voice.

"Where did you go?"

"Nowhere." He tipped the rest of the water down the sink.

"Hugh? I'm worried about you." He shuffled around the sticky kitchen floor, opening drawers and looking for painkillers. "I don't want you bringing people here in the middle of the night. I feel like I'm losing my mind with things being moved and- and strange noises at all hours. Please."

"Where's Dylan?"

"He's in bed, isn't he?"

Hugh paused as he took in this information, and then dashed from the room on his unwilling legs. He took three stairs at a time, his chest protesting with a fierce ache at every forward lunge. Bursting into Dylan's room he found him, as told, in his bed.

"Dylan? Dylan wake up, it's morning."

He put a hand on his brother's shoulder and shook, trying to rouse him; it cupped within his palm. Dylan's head lolled with Hugh's shakes, but he didn't wake. His face was a picture of utter peace. His eyelids were closed like a thin membrane veil. His lips, slightly parted, marked the small o gateway for his soft breath to flow in and out as gentle as displaced air from the flap of a sparrow's wing.

Hugh shook him again, now gripping both shoulders as he applied enough force to lift him off the pillow. But as soon as he ceased, Dylan sunk back into immobility.

"Dylan!" he shouted, but his voice broke and cracked. He studied his brother's chest, seeing it rise and fall. He was at a loss. Dylan never slept beyond nine, usually not beyond sunrise. But last night had not been usual.

He left the house in a hurry, putting his aches and pains to the back of his mind. His mother called something as he shut the door, but he didn't pause. He let out only a brief shiver as he passed beneath the trees, keeping his eyes down as he took the shortcut to the clearing.

"Gamel? I need to speak to you, it's urgent." he called, projecting his still damaged voice best he could across the water.

He waited a few minutes to give Gamel a chance to come, pacing around and kicking dirt. When he'd decided enough time had passed, he raised his chin and looked around once more. Gamel was not there. Hugh strode to the trees where

Gamel liked to eat. He shoved branches aside and looked around where he and Dylan had built the den, but he was still alone.

He took a deep breath.

"Listen to me. I don't know what you've done to my brother but he won't wake up. Hear me? You don't mess around with him. If you've done something you better undo it right now."

The birds had quietened as if in respect for his monologue, and around him the air felt heavy, as if the whole woodland was listening.

"What happened last night? Why save me if you're going to leave me like this?"

He was still alone. High on a distant branch, a bird chirped up its merry call. *What if he doesn't wake up? What if it's because of me?*

On the far river bank he finally saw some movement. It was Sanna. She stood facing him, her head high and proud. Only her tail swished as she stood and watched. Hugh felt a sweep of anger wash over him as this creature stared at him with no idea of the damage, the worry and the pain she had caused. He bent and picked up a thick stick from the ground. With one smooth movement he launched it in her direction. He wasn't aiming to strike her with it and knew the arc of its flight would peak long before reaching her, but he would do anything to stop those piercing black eyes from fixing him with that disturbing intelligence she possessed, like a scientist examining a lower creature for study or a predator observing its prey.

It had the desired effect. As the stick departed from his hand, Sanna moved with lightning speed. Her head tossed in anger and her hooves kicked up clods of mud as they spun and sent her galloping away. She was gone. He stared at the spot where she had just been until a voice from behind made him jump.

"It'd be wise to treat her with some respect lad." said a deep, disapproving voice. Gamel was next to him. He looked tired and aged, slightly stooped, as if a heavy burden was drawing from the bare youth that he had.

"Did you hear what I said?"

"I did." Gamel replied.

"I can't wake my brother." The anger was fading now, leaving desperation in its trail.

"It's undone. You will be able to wake him if he is not already."

Hugh looked over his shoulder toward home, as if he could see through the trees and the vast space.

"You better not have hurt him."

Gamel made a slow shake of his head, his cap propped at a jaunty angle.

"I never would. I just brought on a deep sleep so I could make sure you would be ok. I forgot to undo it before I left, and for that I'm sorry. You should be resting."

Hugh looked down and closed his eyes. The adrenaline and worry for his brother that had taken priority over his pain was leaving him, and as a result the ache of his joints and the awful stuffiness in his head and chest were coming crashing back. Gamel looked concerned, but moved no closer.

"I don't understand what happened." he said, trying to hold back tears. "I was trying to find somewhere for Sanna and you."

"Sanna saved you. She pulled you from the water."

"Why? That's what I don't understand."

"Because you're different. For some reason she's bonded with you. Maybe she senses something in you, something that is not like the others."

"But she's a monster." He hid his face in his hands. The weariness from the night before seemed to have broken down his strength.

"What makes you say that?"

"She killed that man."

No further word passed between them for a few minutes. Hugh sat and let out the tears he'd been holding back. Gamel sat and watched the river, his right hand absently stroking the log on which he sat. Sanna had returned to the water. She stood like a painting, unbothered by flying insects or the floating pollen.

"Don't lie." Hugh said. "She killed him, didn't she?"

"I can't say-"

"Please." he interrupted. "Don't lie to me."

"It's unfortunate, that's what she has to do to survive. It is her instinct."

"That's what you said before, but it still doesn't explain much. It doesn't explain what she is."

Gamel sighed. He looked at Hugh like he was searching for something. He seemed to find what he was looking for.

"I told you she was part of folklore where we're from. It's more than that; she's part of my heritage. In times long ago, people were familiar with those of her kind. In rural areas, anywhere with deep water, people would tell stories of a lone, white horse that would stand by the water's edge. The horse would lure people onto its back and then run into the water and drown them before they could escape. It was more than a horse. Like I said, most local people were familiar with the danger, but that didn't stop travelers or children going missing from time to time. "

"So she is a monster."

"She most certainly is not. She's a damn sight more intelligent and complex than a good many of the people I've had the misfortune to meet. She is not so primitive as a simple monster." He pulled a face at having to say the word. "I have watched her man the hills and the water's edges in both driving wind and battering rain, through the harshest of winters. Like a shepherd to the lost, or rather, the damned. She is part of this world as much as you and I."

Hugh wiped at his face with the sleeves of his hoodie. From the river, Sanna stared towards him. Her nostrils flared as she watched for any more incoming sticks.

"She saved you." Gamel said. "Despite what she is, she chose to save your life."

"Maybe I didn't want to be saved." he managed to say, every word scraping in his throat.

"You listen. I don't want any of that talk from you. And I don't want you to go wandering around at night by yourself either, far from home."

"It was better than being in that house." He was studying the wear of his jeans at the knee where the denim had come apart and faded with age. "What is it exactly that she is, what are they called?"

"I can't say. Not while she is here. Another time and I'll tell you."

"Gamel? What other powers do you have? I know you can disappear, and you can make people sleep, like Dylan."

"Powers." Gamel scoffed. He spat at the leaves around his feet. "If I need to, I can hide from sight. If necessary, I can get inside locked places. If it's required, on a rare occasion, I can influence people, physically." Hugh's eyes widened. Gamel caught sight of his expression. "That is no more than you already knew. I should be more careful."

"I want to know."

"No more questions. You need to rest."

Hugh stood; his body was no less painful for having sat down.

"I might have found somewhere for you. There's a disused

building at the local lake reserve, right by the water."

Gamel buffed the air between them with one hand.

"Recover first, then we'll worry about that. Get back to your brother, back to your bed."

After a mumbled goodbye, Hugh headed home. It was true, he desperately needed the warmth and the chance to recuperate, but his mind was anything but at rest.

Dylan was in the kitchen, searching for a clean cup. Without speaking, Hugh went straight to him and dropped to hug him. Nothing felt better than the life and warmth between his arms. His brother clutched against his chest.

"Hugh? Hugh, I want a drink."

"Ok buddy." He wiped his red eyes with one rough sweep of his sleeve. "I love you."

In his room, he phoned Liana. He had no answer on her mobile, but deciding he had waited long enough, tried the house phone. It was her mum who answered. He asked for her, trying to sound polite and well-mannered despite the husk in his voice.

"Hello?"

"It's me. How come you didn't answer your phone?"

"Oh." She sounded flustered. "I was just sorting through my clothes. I must have missed it."

"Did you get to check out that place yesterday?"

"Yes, I did. Sorry, I was meant to report back to you, wasn't I. I got distracted." She laughed briefly, sounding more nervous than light-hearted. "It seems pretty good. It looks like an old bike shelter or small shed or something. It's a bit cluttered but it's sturdy enough for someone to set up home in, I guess."

"Clutter's not an issue."

"Hugh, what's wrong with your voice?"

"It's nothing."

"Are you sure? Sounds like you're in a bad way."

"Yeah, it's just a cold, no big deal. What else can you tell me about this place, is it quiet?"

"It's really quiet; you can't even see it until you come through this thick set of trees. The water isn't far from it either. Just down this long slope."

"Sounds great. I need to get over there and have a look. Do you have that printout yet?"

"Yeah, I have it here. My sister will be able to give us a lift, maybe in a few days?"

"No problem, just make sure it's in the evening please. I'll come pick up the map in the morning."

"Ok." she said in a small voice. He heard her breathe in, as if on the cusp of saying more, but the line was silent.

"I'm gonna get a drink." he said.

"Sounds like you need it. See you tomorrow."

It was the following afternoon. A bright sun was overhead and Hugh relished its bright warmth on his pale and freckled arms. In one hand he carried a new carrier bag of meat from Ben, swinging it with every stride. In his pocket was the map from Liana. It was all coming together. He walked with purpose, his trainers slapping against the sun-scorched pavement that led to his house. The last of the village at this end, set apart from the others. At the top of a winding hill where all could speculate, but none could get a close look at. The road was quiet and empty. Somewhere far above an airplane took strangers high and far away, and down here on this quiet road, in this quiet part of the village, he had done what he had set out to do.

The house was in sight. From this distance it looked well

maintained. A spacious home. From a nearby garden, the sound of a lawnmower sprung up.

"Hugh!" A familiar voice shouted him from behind. He looked over his shoulder and saw Kain. He set his head down and picked up his pace. "Don't try to get away, wait up!"

"I'm not interested in arguments." he replied. He scrunched the handles of the bag into his fist. Kain caught up with him and sidestepped in front of Hugh to block his path.

"Just let me see what's in the bag."

"Why do you care so much?"

"Because I want to know what's got you, Liana and Ben all acting so weird. You can't just shut me out."

"It's just something for my mum, ok? Let me get home." Hugh tried to walk around him but found his way blocked again, he kept his eyes down and his hand tightly closed.

"Listen. We used to be good mates. Just let me in on what's going on. I know it's something. Show me what's in the bag and we can move on from all this."

"Are you going to apologise?"

"For what? The party? It was nothing."

Hugh used his shoulder to push past him. He got in front, but it was seconds before a firm hand gripped his upper arm.

"Get off me. Just leave it."

"You've got a thing for Liana, is that what this is about? You want to get her interested in you, push me out the picture."

"You're wrong."

"Am I? I spoke to her earlier, you know. You can't keep me away."

Hugh pulled away from Kain and struggled to free his arm. To his surprise, Kain let go and watched him walk away. Hugh readjusted his misshapen hoodie with a quick shrug and tried to focus on getting home, getting indoors. He kept his gaze fixed on the monotony of the grey concrete at his feet, waiting and wishing for it to break off to his right so he could step onto the crumbling, weedy drive that led to his house.

He heard steps coming from behind. With no time to turn or react, the air was displaced from his lungs and the ground rushed towards his face with startling speed. Kain had shoved him to the ground and on falling, he had dropped the bag. He was trying to get himself back up with scraped palms. He saw Kain scoop up the bag, tipping out its contents with a bemused expression.

"What's this?" Kain said with a frown. He used his foot to turn over the clear wrapped package of raw meat parts, waste cuts and offal. "What's so secret about this that Liana and Ben can know and not me?"

Hugh stood up, feeling a little dazed. He put the meat back into the bag and faced Kain.

"They're real friends. Not like you."

He turned his back on Kain and carried on towards his house. His knees and his palms and his head hurt from the fall, but he wouldn't run.

"There's something wrong with you, Hugh." Kain called. "You're not normal."

"I don't want you to leave." Hugh said. He was looking at the map in Gamel's deeply lined and bulbous fingers. In his deep study, Gamel's head tilted down and his eyes seemed to shrink amongst the sagging skin of his face as he squinted. His breathing was slight and quick, and Hugh could pick out the small details of his woolen cap sprung with wayward threads, the scars and the red capillaries that flushed his sallow cheeks. Gamel looked up at him.

"I'll be sad to go. But you can't want me hanging around forever, a young lad like you with your whole life ahead of you.

I've spent my life. I want to settle and never move, lie quietly and stop ever having to worry about our future again."

"But you're my friend."

"As you are mine, and always will be."

Sanna stood alert on the opposite bank, watching the trees. She blew through her nostrils, the whites of her eyes visible.

"Since you came, it's made a big difference. Normally I'd just be inside all the time, avoiding people. Having you to talk to and helping with the house, having something to look forward to, I've actually been happy, or getting there. I feel like I've got something to live for again, other than looking after my brother."

"Is this because of your mum you were feeling like that?"

Hugh let his head drop and put his hands between his knees.

"Probably. She isn't there for me. It doesn't feel like she cares."

"That's her illness though. I'm sure that she cares."

"Well, why can't she get better for us then?" He looked straight at Gamel. "I'm not angry at you I'm just angry. She won't change."

Gamel prodded the small fire with a stick, turning the embers to reveal their white hot and crumbling undersides.

"We have to believe things will change. Even people." He passed the stick to Hugh, who studied its charred end. "Sometimes we have to put faith in others and know that none of us can be perfect. Your mother is battling her own personal demons. I don't think that means she doesn't care."

"The other night she didn't even pick up on what had happened. I don't think she'll change until she realises how bad it is and how it's making me feel. But I can't speak to her about it."

Gamel's lips twitched and he looked to be deep in thought. Hugh had been so distracted by their conversation, he'd

forgotten about Sanna. A sudden whinny brought her to his
attention again. He raised his head to see her cantering
towards them, crossing the water and the clearing within a few
seconds. Gamel reached out his hand, making quiet
clucking noises in his throat. Her mane had been carefully
arranged in a long running plait, and her tail was braided right
to the end.

"She seems a lot better." Hugh said.

"She is. She's getting her strength back."

Hugh pulled a pen from his pocket.

"I brought this, so you can write what Sanna is rather than
have to say it."

Gamel's brow morphed into deep lines. He squinted at the
pen, squeezing its narrow, smooth casing with his thick, rough
fingers.

"I'm not good at writing."

"It's ok." Hugh replied. He watched while Gamel laboured
over the clear side of the map. He couldn't see what was being
written, only his hunched figure, the stiff movement of his
hand. Gamel sat up again and frowned at what he'd written
before passing it to Hugh.

Hugh looked at a foreign word that he didn't recognise.

Nykur

His lips moved as if to form the sound and Gamel shushed
him with a reproaching look.

"Don't speak it." he said. Hugh nodded and glanced at Sanna.
She peered down at him with her alert, black eyes.

"C'mon, forlade." Gamel said to Sanna, shooing her with his
hands. She pivoted on the spot and galloped back to the water.

"Can you tell me what you are?" Hugh asked.

"I can tell you, but it would be easier for me to write."

Hugh waited again whilst Gamel wrote. He studied the word.

"Tomte?" Gamel nodded.

"Not that it means anything to you I'm sure. We were, like Sanna, quite commonplace at one time. My old home was where I spent my whole life. I looked after the farm and the animals there, and was respected by each family I served until, gradually, things changed."

"What things?"

"In those early years, I would receive payment as it were, in food and lodging. My service and protection was highly valued. Then modern machines came and changed the whole landscape. Where I was previously given space and warm porridge, I know found my home cleared out with no regard to me, and people that were quick, loud, like their machines. It is modernisation." He said the word slowly, feeling his way around it. "It is no longer taking time or respect for old skills and culture, but churning everything up with mechanical claws."

"So you came here?"

Gamel dipped his head, an almost imperceptible nod. His left hand moved to his pocket and reached inside the narrow gap to feel the edge of age-worn paper. His breathing quickened.

"Yes, we came here, hoping for a better life."

"I hope I can help you find it. Maybe this place will be it. I just wish you could stay."

Hugh walked the dark path towards home, passing under the trees with his head down. He heard the snap of broken sticks behind him.

"Hello?" Though his sight had adjusted to the dark, he still struggled to distinguish between the bleak shapes of the woods. He heard something approaching, soft thuds on the carpet of leaves. It was Sanna. She came toward him like a pale ghost, so stark and smooth was her appearance and movement. He thought of her leaving and not coming back. He let his chin rest on his chest, trying to hold back tears.

A gust of cold breath hit the back of his neck. She was right behind him. He turned and held the smooth flat of her cheeks in his hands, letting her head press into his chest. They stood that way for what felt like a long time. Though Sanna was so close and he could feel her gentle breathing, there was no warmth from her to keep the cold from settling in his hands and feet. He pulled away. Under her watch, he returned to the house.

Chapter 12

They were sat in the back of the small car, watching through the windows as the evening set in outside.

"It's along this road." Liana said. "There should be a sign for the footpath." Hugh saw her sister glance at them both in the rearview. "It's only a short walk."

Hugh was quiet as her sister pulled into the small side road, that ended abruptly with railings and a small gap where the footpath began. He unbuckled.

"Don't get into any kind of trouble." Liana's sister said as they got out.

"Are you ok? You look pale." Liana said.

"I'm fine, let's get going."

The path was so narrow that Liana had to walk behind him. They picked their way along the track, concentrating on their feet. The path began to open out among sparse trees, and Hugh could see the body of water up ahead.

"It's just around the next bend." Liana said a little breathlessly. There was a crashing sound from up ahead, like a wooden crate being smashed, followed by laughter. Hugh stopped and looked over his shoulder for Liana. She stood a few meters back, her face fixed with worry.

"Hugh-" she started.

"What is it?"

"Maybe we should go back." As he went to her, she avoided his eye contact. "Don't be upset with me."

"Are there people there?"

"Kain kept pushing and pushing to know what was happening. I told him we were coming here to see if it would be any good for your friend."

"What did you tell him about Gamel? About the horse?"

Liana's eyes were wide. She stumbled over her words when

she spoke.

"Not a lot. Hugh?"

He turned away and carried on walking towards the noise. At the treeline, he could see the outbuilding in a small clearing that was well hidden from the main path. It stood on its own patch of ground, shielded by trees, with only a small campfire set up outside. Beyond that, the ground sloped towards a large lake that filled much of the landscape.

He came through the trees and stopped to catch his breath. A familiar figure was standing by the propped open door.

"Ben?" Hugh said.

"Hey." Ben greeted him with a slap on the shoulder. "Kain said you might be coming."

"Where is he?" Ben nodded towards the inside of the building.

The interior was crumbling and rotting, an abandoned place. The last of the daylight came through the gutted roof in patches and the walls were grey with broken brick and cobwebs hanging heavy with dust.

"There you are." Kain appeared from behind a low, cracked wall. His friend Michael stumbled behind him. "Do you like what we've done with the place?" He gestured to a large wooden pallet board that had been straightened and raised on some bricks. At one end was a discarded metal chair they'd found, at its side was an upturned bucket and what looked like a rusted tin of oil. "That's the dining table. We're making it a right little home. The kind of home you wanted for your friend, right?"

"Why are you here Kain, why d'you care so much?"

Kain dropped the piece of brick he'd been holding and got close to Hugh.

"To prove a point; I told you I'd find out. What's so special about your friend that you needed to keep it from me?" Liana stepped through the doorway, looking at both of them anxiously. "You lied to me." Kain pointed his finger, the nail stained with nicotine. "Why? You didn't think I could help? Or am I just so beneath you."

"There's no need to argue." Liana said.

Kain shuffled closer to Hugh, so close that he could smell his cigarette breath.

"I don't want to fight with you, or argue. I never have." Hugh said. "No-one was meant to know about it."

"Well, she told me." Kain said in a low voice. "Only took a bit of pressure for her to spill." He turned and addressed the room. "What I really want to know is what Ben's part is in all this, 'cos he won't give anything away."

Kain sent an empty can skidding across the dusty floor with his toe. At the door, Ben looked in on the scene, his skin an unhealthy ashen colour. Hugh could feel his cheeks flushing red.

"Just leave it please, there's nothing more for you to find out."

"Yeah? What's his name then?" Hugh's stayed silent. His feet felt fixed to the grimy floor. "What's with the horse? Is he some kind of freak?"

"Shut up!" Hugh exploded into movement. He shot forwards, shoving Kain back with both hands on his shoulders. Liana got between them, trying to block Kain as he regained his balance. In the background there was indistinct shouting from Ben whilst Michael watched, slack mouthed.

Hugh went outside, shrugging past Ben and relishing in the cold wind that hit him. He could leave the chaos behind him, though he knew it wouldn't last for long. For a brief few moments he could breathe in the evening air, whipped from the water's surface and carrying the cool scent of the world around him. Though the water was peaceful, his mind retained the former chaos that had driven him outside. Liana had betrayed him. No-one was supposed to know and yet now the secret was out. He had betrayed Gamel. With good intentions maybe, but the fact remained the same. He let himself drop onto a vacant log by the fire. He wished that no-one could ever follow him; that he himself could disappear rather than own up to the trouble he'd caused. He watched through tired and half-closed eyes as the burgeoning fire licked at the dry wood pile. He tried to make himself small, curling over on himself and allowing his head to drop, hoping that he couldn't be seen, couldn't be engaged with.

Behind him he heard more crashing and loud shouts, sounds of high spirits rather than anger. His mood sunk even lower. He was immune to the nip of the wind at his bare ears and hands, the dull cramp in his knees and the growing ache at his neck. He welcomed physical discomfort.

The sound of footsteps came near. A plump hand touched his shoulder.

"You alright?" A gruff voice said. Ben sat next to him, picking up a stick and prodding at the fire. "Don't stress about it too much. It's no big deal."

"It is a big deal. It's a big deal to me."

There was a pause and the rustle of plastic packaging as Ben took a packet of marshmallows from a carrier bag on the ground. Without thought to any dirt, he squashed one onto his stick and watched it soften and turn black in the small flame, breathing through his open mouth.

"He trusted me and I've let him down," Hugh said, consumed with the dark nature of his thoughts.

"Maybe he'll understand. Kain tried it with me. I said no from the start but he kept asking, tried to pressure me. I was never goin' to tell him anythin'." He tested the toasted marshmallow with his lips before taking a tentative bite.

"Kain'll forget about it, it's no biggie.

There was a loud bang from behind them, the door of the building rebounding off the wall with violent force. Kain, Michael and Liana joined them by the fire. Kain sat close to Liana, reaching for the other carrier bags and laying out an array of beer and snacks.

"No reason why we can't still have a party," he said, selecting some music to play from his phone. Michael picked up a beer and offered it to Hugh who shook his head. Kain cracked one open and drained half of it in a few noisy gulps.

"I need a piss." Michael said, looking around for a suitable spot.

"Go round the back of the building. We don't want to watch." Kain said. Michael shuffled off with a grunt, disappearing behind the wall.

"Loosen up." Kain said to Liana. "You're as bad as Hugh." He put one arm around her waist and pulled her tense frame close to him, planting a rough kiss on her cheek. Hugh glanced at her and saw she was watching him. Her whole face was tight with worry and guilt. He looked away. There was a glint in Kain's eyes.

"Trust you to be scoffing those," he said to Ben. He slapped his legs in time with the music.

Michael reappeared looking pale and frightened. He ran towards them, one hand fumbling with his fly.

"What now." Kain said.

"I saw something back there. In the trees, something watching me."

Kain silenced his phone with the press of a button.

"Show me." The two of them stalked off, Kain taking the lead, leaving the others by the fire. Ben sat between Hugh and Liana, oblivious to the awkward undercurrent.

"Hugh-" Liana said, trying to attract his gaze. "I'm sorry, let me explain-"

"Leave me alone." He sat, unmoving, refusing to look in her direction. After a silent minute, she got up and followed Kain and Michael. Hugh stayed where he was for as long as he could bear, desperate to move and to shake off his thoughts. He stood.

"You coming?" he said to Ben.

"Nah." Ben was still occupied with the marshmallows. He'd managed to fit three on a stick and seemed to be testing just how hot he could get them before they dropped off the stick as a gooey black mass.

Hugh went after where the others had headed, watching his feet sink into the damp grass with each step. He found them behind the building. Kain was brandishing a thick branch, sweeping it around where the open space fell away to thick shrubs and trees. After a minute of this he threw it, javelin style, into the black undergrowth.

"Tell me again, what was it you saw?" Kain said.

"A face." Michael said, shrinking back against the crumbling wall. "The eyes, they were, like, watching."

"So it was just some animal then you useless lump."

"No, it was human, I think. I looked round and it was there, in the trees."

Kain scanned the tree line again with a critical eye.

"Well, there's nothing there now. Let's get back. I want my beer." He passed Hugh deliberately close, shouldering him out of the way. "You reckon it's your friend come to say hi?" he called back over his shoulder.

They returned to an empty campfire. The blackened stick Ben had been using was discarded on the ground.

"Where's he gone?" Kain said. They looked around, confused by his absence until Liana's hands rushed to her face.

"He's in the water," she gasped.

Hugh looked towards the lake and his heart froze at what he saw. Ben was facing away from them, already up to his knees in the lake. Further in, Sanna was lying down, the water rising over her flanks and creeping up her neck. From the movement of Ben's broad back away from them, he knew he was trying to reach her.

The three of them ran down the slope towards him.

"Ben?" Kain shouted. "What are you playing at? Get out the water!"

Ben turned and looked at them, his eyes like round discs in the soft moon of his face. Hugh felt sick, knowing that beneath the water, the silty mud would be creeping over Ben's shoes.

"It's drowning." Ben said. "I've got to help."

Sanna's head dipped and rolled above the water surface, restless and disturbed by her bursts of wild thrashing. To an unsuspecting eye, she appeared to be an animal out of its habitat, stuck and distressed and fighting for its life. Hugh was struck cold by the usual, impassionate black of her eyes. When still, she monitored Ben's movements far closer than that of her own predicament.

"Ben-" Hugh said, "Come back now, it's dangerous."

"How're you going to rescue it, anyway?" Kain said. "You can hardly pull it out."

"I don't know, the way it was looking at me. I had to try to do something. It's dying."

"If you get out the water, we can deal with it." Hugh said. Liana was fussing at his arm, trying to get his attention but he ignored her.

"My feet are stuck. It's like quicksand." Ben said, and now panic began to grip his face. Hugh slipped off his trainers and raised a foot to enter the lake. He felt the strong grip of Kain on his arm.

"Stay out of there or we'll all get stuck." Kain turned and

looked for Michael. He was slack mouthed, holding his phone up to video Ben. Kain strode over and slapped the phone from his hands, letting it fall into the long grass. His voice was low and urgent. "Run back up there and look for some rope, if not, something long like a branch or a pole."

As Michael lumbered breathlessly back up the hill and Kain searched the uneven ground for something useful, Hugh turned to Liana.

"What's she doing? Is she drowning?" she said. Hugh shook his head, frowning. "What'll happen? Don't you know anything we can do?"

She looked over his shoulder towards the shadowy summit of the hill, where a short time ago mixed spirits and the warm campfire had presided. "Is your friend here?" she whispered.

Kain overheard her. He straightened with the slow quality of someone more occupied with the whirring of their mind, the connecting of thoughts.

"She's not drowning!" Liana called to Ben. "She's fine in the water."

"You know that do you?" Kain said. Liana looked at him, her tense shoulders trembling slightly. She glanced towards the bank.

In the lake, the water frothed and splashed as Sanna began to struggle again. The whites of her eyes flashed around their dark centers. The violent movement of her head and writhing body sent great tumultuous swells past Ben and towards the bank where the rest of them watched helplessly.

Ben renewed his efforts to free his foot, but lost his balance. Leaving his shoe stuck in the mire of the soft lake bed, he went forwards towards Sanna in some dim hope she could still be rescued and as the closest thing he could hold on to. She was still a few meters away, but the sound of her splashing was louder to him than the shouts from the bank. He hit the deep water, struggling to work his arms and legs in what felt and appeared like thick murkiness around him.

Hugh felt helpless as he watched with Kain red faced by his side. Ben tried to swim, his legs now free but weighted by his clothes. He watched how Sanna changed. As Ben got within touching distance, her struggles stopped. She went still, as though she had shut down. Ben reached for her like a lifeguards ring, groping for her head and neck. At his touch, Sanna's wild and rolling eyes went still, fixing him in her gaze. He took her sodden neck and mane in a grappling bear hug, trying to both pull her landwards and keep himself above the water's surface.

On the bank, the boys hesitated. Michael rejoined them holding a long branch.

"Hugh, you need to do something." Liana said. He studied the water's edge again, indecision plaguing him. He looked back at Sanna and hoped with every fibre that she wouldn't hurt Ben. He remembered how she had come to him on that dark night when he'd been drowning and had taken his weight, pulling him to safety with ease. She was like a statue now. Not the violent creature that Liana feared.

Ben relaxed and let her hold his weight. He waited until his breathing slowed and his strength returned, but when he went to move his hand, he realised he could not easily pry his fingers from her skin. His hands were stuck to the horse, as if a seal had formed between his skin and the smooth surface of her coat.

"What's going on?" Kain shouted from the shoreline.

"I'm stuck again." Ben's voice was breathless and faint. "I can't-"

He trailed off, his face pressed close to Sanna, watching them with a bewildered expression, pockmarked skin, the slight pucker of his mouth. In some portion of his brain, he must have known the danger he was in, that he was in the clutch of an apex predator.

Sanna regarded him with calm sentience, he that was fixed to her neck and smelled of algae and fear. Then she rolled with lethal speed, pulling him over her and plunging deep into the darkness of the lake.

Hugh watched Ben disappear in a rolling motion under the water. He rushed into the lake with no thought now for Kain or for the sinking ground or Liana's frantic crying.

"Give me that." Kain grabbed the branch from Michael's hands and went in after Hugh. They were both scrambling to get to where Ben had gone under and where the surface was alive like water come to the boil. Kain grabbed onto Hugh with his free arm, pushing past him and through the sticking riverbed. He dived forwards, making a plunge for the deep water.

Sanna breached the surface with a toss of her head, taking in Kain's presence now only a few feet away, where he lunged for her with the branch. Ben resurfaced, white with fear and struggling for breath. While Sanna was distracted by the blows of the branch, not yet on her but coming ever closer, Hugh put all his effort into reaching Ben, stretching through the water though it dragged and resisted him. Ben saw him and started to close the gap between them. But Sanna spun with ease despite the deep water, turning her haunches towards Kain and placing Ben at her front. Before Hugh had time to react, Sanna brought her bared teeth down on top of Ben, bearing down on him with the weight of her chest and front legs as he crumpled beneath her and was lost again.

Kain was close enough to reach her with the branch, striking at where he could see her. She raised her head and tried to turn on him in her own defence, but Kain was ready. He hit her on the head, by the temple, the full weight of the wood striking her hard.

"Grab him! Grab Ben!" Kain shouted at Hugh, who felt so lost and helpless as if stuck in a bad dream. Sanna moved out of Kain's reach, shaking her head as if to try to rid her pain. The sight of Kain's curled, blood-red lips and his lank, black hair stuck to him with the effort of what he'd done startled Hugh back into action. He pushed forward, trying to feel for his friend, trying to grope for his soft form in that which could not be seen, dead man's hands. He was spluttering for air, trying not to panic at the feel of the water wrapping round his neck.

"There!" Kain shouted. Hugh looked to where he gestured and saw the curled white shape of Ben's hand, risen above the surface. Hugh took Ben's hand, getting a good enough grip of his upper body so he could pull his head out of the water. His eyes were closed and his face was bloodless.

"Keep her away," he called vaguely over his shoulder to Kain, but he was by his side.

"Just get him out." Kain said. Together they pulled Ben towards dry land and the others. Kain kept his body facing toward Sanna, keeping the branch held high and ready. They got to the shallows and Michael and Liana met them, lifting Ben together and laying him on his back in the long, coarse grass.

"Call an ambulance," Hugh said, smoothing Ben's wet hair and bending over his mouth in the hope that he would feel some soft flutter of breath.

In the lake, Sanna came within a few metres of the bank, sodden and wild. She pawed at the water, her neck bowed and her mouth tight.

"Is he alive?" Liana asked, her face streaked with tears and her voice altered by shock.

"I don't know." Hugh said coarsely. He took a hold of Ben's wrist, his skin slippery and cold. After a few seconds of pressing with his thumb, he felt the faint throb of a pulse.

"He's alive," he said, but Liana was busy on the phone. With some effort he rolled Ben towards one side, hitting his back between the shoulder blades, pleading for him to wake up. His hand made a sickening sound against his drenched clothes, the impact sounding as if it hit a hollow cavity rather than the chest of one of his most trusted friends, capable of exploding in deep, booming laughter or enveloping him in hugs so tight that he felt sometimes he would be crushed. Now it seemed like an empty thing.

Kain took a rock from Michael. The size of a plum, he rolled it in his palm. Sanna stood with her head lowered, lower than the level of her back. Her eyes spoke black nothings in the night, her gaze a cursive charm. Fat droplets of water fell from her mane and into the lake from which they birthed. He closed his fingers and drew back his arm, ready to throw. Her head jerked upwards, her ears coming to sharp white points beneath the black sky.

With a grunt of effort he threw the rock at her. She whirled in a furious reaction, her tail swishing in anger as it glanced off her hock. He paused, watching to see what she did. Sanna turned back to face him and stood as she was before. She would not give up her challenge or break the direct stare that angered him so much.

"Get me more rocks," he said to Michael. Taking another one he launched it with a powerful over arm swing. It struck her neck. She reared up, lashing and kicking. As she came back down another rock hit the front of her chest.

"Stop that. Stop hurting her," Hugh said, still crouched by Ben.

"You-" Kain began, a low menace in his voice. Hugh got to his feet, anticipating an attack when a strange voice interrupted them.

"If you do anything to that horse again, you're going to

regret it, you better believe me." Gamel was approaching them from the top of the bank. The long grass came to the top of his legs. "You'll have one square between the eyes if you so much as look at another rock."

"Who are you?" Kain said. His eyes set in a shrewd, piercing expression. He squared his feet and watched the old man come closer with slow and steady steps. "And what in hell's business is it of yours old man?"

The clouded night sky was a muted black, making it hard for any of them to make out more than the man's stout shadow of a figure. He was hunched over, his hands hanging like weights at his side. His woolen cap gave him a strange silhouette in the dark.

Hugh was consumed with nervous energy and a desperate sense of guilt. As Gamel came ever closer to them, his face obscured by the lack of light and the slight dip of his chin, he feared what would happen. Kain looked between Hugh and the old man, a knowing smile creeping across his face.

"You're Hugh's new friend," he said with a leer, "The freak-" his words cut off abruptly as his whole face and body stiffened. "What's happening?"

"Walk to the water." Gamel ordered, his voice low and assertive.

Kain's face seemed to contort as the outer sign of an intense inner struggle.

"Gamel, please-" Hugh said.

"You stay right where you are boy," Gamel said without looking at him. "Walk to the water," he repeated. He met Kain's glare with calm authority.

Kain turned stiffly, his feet lagging. He went to the water's edge with his arms by his sides, Gamel smiling as he watched.

"Stop!" Kain shouted, as if with great effort. But his feet kept moving, his shoes now intercepting the break of the lake water against dry land.

"Going swimming boy?" Gamel said. Kain seemed to tremble for a second and then dropped to his knees as though his legs had been kicked from behind.

"Don't hurt him! What are you doing?" Liana said, still clutching her phone. Michael watched with an open mouth.

In the water, Sanna stood watching Kain as the lake began to saturate his clothes further. Her head was high and alert. Her white, slender legs seemed to grow out of the calm water as if she were part of it, and the wet tangle of her usually brushed mane and tail was the only sign of her previous unrest. She crept forward, her movements almost imperceptible. She was like a silent, equine wraith of the lake; and she was focused on Kain.

Kain began to struggle, his movements constrained but erratic. He shuffled on his knees into the deeper water.

Hugh was watching, his heart torn between the plight of Kain and Ben. Liana got in front of him and commanded his attention.

"Do something, you've got to, he's your friend."

"I can't"

"You have to. There must be something."

With an effort he let his eyes settle on Liana's face. He placed a hand on her arm, squeezing just a little.

"There is nothing-" he paused, his voice breaking. "Nothing, that I can do. You don't understand."

The wail of a siren was coming closer.

"It's the ambulance, for Ben," he called to Gamel.

Gamel turned, letting Kain slump. The siren was getting louder. He stepped past Kain and strode into the shallows. A silent communication seemed to pass between him and the horse.

"Komme," he said. Sanna ducked beneath the surface and

disappeared from view. He stooped to pick something up, putting the white object into his pocket. Without further word or glance, Gamel walked back past the group of them and ascended the hill.

Kain got to his feet on trembling legs. As he approached, he avoided looking into anyone's face, instead trying to wring out the waterlogged legs of his jeans. His hands were shaking. Michael stepped in front of him.

"You alright mate?"

Kain shoved him aside and went straight to Hugh. He took the front of his top with both hands, twisting and pulling the material towards him. His face was inches away.

"That freak you call a friend will pay for this. You see if he doesn't."

He was trapped in Kain's grip. He looked into his pale grey face, mute with shock. Kain's hands trembled against the fabric of his top and they finally relented, letting him loose as the siren reached a crescendo and the glare of lights came into view. Kain left them, and Ben did not wake.

Chapter 13

Hugh took to his bed cold and weary. He'd held himself together by the lakeside, watching as the paramedics worked over his friend. Despite the people, the touching, the equipment; Even when he was on the stretcher and taken inside the ambulance with its white and clinical inside, Ben did not open his eyes.

His face had felt like stone. His mouth felt as though it would never speak again. The world passed outside the windows of the car and he felt disconnected from his own body, from the feel of the cushioned seats and the sound of Liana's faraway voice. It was only when the back door clicked shut and he knew he was alone that he was released. Sound escaped his mouth and his body began to shake. He could feel the cold wet stiffness of his jeans and the dull ache in his forehead was suddenly all consuming.

He made it to his bedroom and found the comfort of his quilt as it sunk around him. Yet sleep would not come. What had he done? What was set in motion? In his mind, every worry was framed around his own actions. The silence of the room seemed to bear down on him and sleep seemed as far away as a hopeful thought, and yet his mind persisted with images, questions.

A noise like the scatter of gun shells made him jump. It was the sound of small stones against his bedroom window. He looked outside and saw Sanna standing in the long grass of the garden. She was waiting by the patio. He slipped on some dry clothes and went to the door, his hands gripping the wood. She lifted her head, her breath was visible in the low light.

Her front hooves struck the cracked paving with a muted thud. He sunk back, holding the door like a shield, not wanting her to come close. He was waiting for Gamel, and at last he appeared from behind Sanna. His face was weary looking. He held his cap in his hands.

"Are you ok lad?" Gamel asked. Hugh nodded.

"I'm sorry-" he started, but had to wipe his eyes with the back of his hand to gain some composure. "I'm so sorry."

"Did you tell them about us?" Gamel asked.

"Only Liana, I thought I could trust her. I just wanted some help, so I didn't let you down." His cheeks were wet again.

Gamel moved towards him, stepping on the patio. His boots were damp and split at the sole. For the briefest of moments Hugh wanted to draw back. A touch of fear passed through him and he instinctively tensed up, putting his weight on his back foot. But Gamel's face had only sympathy and deep sadness. Hugh went to him and found a home in Gamel's arms. The smell of moss and mildew washed over him, the acrid scent of wood smoke and the stiff feel of leather that covered Gamel's shoulders. But Gamel held him, his body beneath his clothing was yielding and warm, offering comfort without words.

They came apart and Hugh felt a desperate panic, like he was on the verge of losing something critical. Gamel seemed to weigh something up in his mind until he cleared his throat to speak.

"Thank you for your help."

"No, don't say you have to leave," Hugh insisted. "There's more I can do, and Ben will be ok. It won't happen again." Gamel looked wary, his small eyes made smaller with the frown of his heavy brow. "I need you here. Seeing you and Sanna is all I look forward to."

"A little while longer, we can stay til then."

Sanna whickered softly and ducked her head. Hugh went to her side, resting his hand on the cool marble of her shoulder.

"What is it?" Gamel said. "You're still not happy."

Hugh wasn't able to stop his flow of tears. He looked down at the uneven paving, spread with weeds.

"I'm just worried about Kain. I don't know what he's capable of."

"I can deal with your friend, if he comes looking."

Hugh looked up at Gamel, who must have picked up on his momentary alarm.

"Not hurt him, just hide. But you know we will have to go someday."

Hugh nodded. "Yeah."

"And you'll be ok when we do."

The next morning brought a bleak and dreary sky that pervaded his bedroom with the same oppressive, murky light. Hugh was on the end of his bed, phone in hand. He was scrolling through the texts sent to Liana since he'd woken this morning, all of which were questions, none of which had replies.

There was a knock at the door from low down. Jack pushed it open and looked in on him.

"Hugh?"

"What is it?" He hid his face.

"Do you want to play?"

"No." He rubbed his eyes with the nubs of his fingers. "Go downstairs."

"But Hugh-"

"Go," he said. His expression was enough to dissuade Dylan from persisting.

A while later Hugh descended the stairs. There was a faint noise from the living room as Dylan quietly occupied himself. In the kitchen, his mother was in the chair by the window, gazing out at the overgrown garden. Her skin was pale and her lips dry and cracking. The skin of her face seemed stretched and fraught.

"Mum?" She looked towards him with blank eyes, her hand staying pressed against her chin as though it needed support still. "I went out last night with some friends. There was an accident."

"I know," she said. She lowered her hand and he saw its trembling as it groped for the chair. "Get me some water, please."

He got a glass from the sink and rinsed it out. He filled it with water to take to her, but as he passed the counter a jumble of colour drew his eye. The magnetic alphabet letters usually strewn across the front of the fridge were scattered on the countertop. Five were set aside from the rest, their arrangement precise and neat, forming a single word. "Janet".

He looked at his mother; The narrow scope of her attention was still on the window.

"What do you know? Have you heard anything about Ben?"

She was silent as he placed the water next to her. Her leathery lips parted and she spoke in a weak voice.

"Accident?" she said.

"Have you heard anything?"

She looked at him directly for the first time in what seemed like many years. It scared him, the intimacy of direct contact with eyes he did not recognise, in a face that he should know above all others.

"What?" he asked.

"Ben's mother called me this morning. He died in hospital last night."

Hugh's face fell slack, and he felt a stab of nausea. He took a step back, his vision blurring with tears.

"Hugh?" she said. "Stay here."

But he was already backing away.

"He's dead?" he asked. It came out like a strangled

statement. He was by the door, half in and half out. His mother stood, her expression one of terror.

"Hugh, please. Stay here with me. Don't leave me alone."

But he was gone. He found the confines of his room and shut the door on the world, his phone forgotten.

He woke from a disturbed sleep with a dry mouth and a stiff neck. The sky outside his window was a black void without stars. In some dark, distant part of his mind he sought water for his throat, painkillers for his head, but on reaching the kitchen he bypassed the sink and went straight to the door. He walked the length of the garden like a spectre, guided not by his physical needs but by the insistence of something else deep within him. It was a place where now only pain resided.

At the clearing, Sanna was waiting for him as if connected. He went to her without pausing to look for Gamel. On the bank, her head lifted and her ears flicked back as he came face to face with her. He was tensed, their eyes were level.

"Why?" Anger came to him like a burgeoning wave. "Why did you do it?"

Sanna dipped her head and took a step back. He got close to her side, taking a fist of mane in his left hand and placing his right against the slope of her back. He dropped his head as hot, angry tears overcame him, but his anger did not subside.

"He was my friend. Why are you like this?" His hands tightened into fists and he pushed her away from him. She yielded, turning to face him and curling her neck.

"Why's this happened?" he shouted, rounding on her again with his shoulders squared to hers. He moved towards her and she lunged at him, quicker than he could react. He felt her teeth take hold of his upper arm and a stab of pain as she bit into his skin with one swift movement. He pulled away, shocked and hurt.

Sanna drew away and dropped forward onto her knees before laying down and settling on the dusty ground. He fell, letting his weight sink towards the dirt beside her. He reached out with his uninjured arm and traced the top of her back where her coat was its smoothest. She pressed her muzzle against his side and he could feel her cold touch permeate through his clothes, cooling his skin. He leant against her, waiting for a reaction. When she nuzzled him again, he climbed onto the breadth of her back, taking a tight hold of her neck.

His world turned skywards. He gripped with his legs as she stood, almost tipping him off her as she rose first with her front end, and then her back with one great effort. She turned towards the water and he tensed in preparation to slide off before the hit of cold water. But she was still. She looked towards the river with an unreadable expression, her breathing slow and steady.

Something caught her attention in the treeline and her head raised, instantly poised to run, quivering like a feather caught in the wind. Hugh let out his breath, the damp cold of her body beginning to chill him. She started forward, and he had no choice but to hold on to her, his hands lost in the thick strands of her mane. She picked up a trot and went straight to the trees, but rather than stop, she picked up speed, finding a path through the dark boughs.

His first instinct was to crouch forwards and press his body to hers, terrified that a stray branch would strike him and tear into his skin or Sanna's sudden swerve would knock him to the ground. But her gallop settled into an even rhythm, and he felt secure against the grip of her coat. He felt no pain and now even fear subsided as only the racing of his heart and the rush of the wind drew into focus as they raced as one through the trees.

He grew brave, letting his upper body come away from her

neck. In front of him, the sight of her flowing mane, pricked ears. The woodland was a black blur that she could navigate without stumbling. He could feel the rhythmic working of her muscles, supple and lean, and the even beat of her hooves as they churned up the soft dirt and leaves. He tried to shout, to scream, but the night air whipped his breath away at first try. He was breathless; without voice, only feeling.

They were coming to the boundary. The light began to change as the trees grew thin and the open space beckoned. He straightened his back and tried to rein her in with his hands and the weight of his body as he leant back and began to brace. The wooden rails of the boundary fence were looming perilously. Sanna seemed to rocket headlong towards them, without regard for her passenger. His elation became fear, waiting for the hit, the fall. A mere few metres away, Sanna swerved violently to the right. It threw Hugh to her left flank, gripping onto her as he tried to avoid falling. She slowed, allowing him to right himself. She lowered her head as she broke into a trot, finding the crest of a hidden bank and descending it to join the river.

He hoped she would stop and give him the chance to dismount, but her speed increased again, the shallow water giving her traction enough on the rocky bed. He looked down and saw only great swathes of murky depths, thrown into a tempest with the crashing of her hooves. He was starting to slip, his body relenting its balance as his view was consumed with the water, the lucid, mire like quality of what he feared. His grip loosened, and in one fluid movement he slipped from her back and met the river.

The shock of the water was a fleeting priority, for when he found resistance enough to right himself, Sanna was above him, her perilous hooves alarmingly close. He pushed back with all his strength, putting distance between them as quickly as he could manage. She bore down on him, her head bobbing towards him, but he threw up the water towards her with his palms. He hit the bank, a safe distance away now as she became still. He fought to regain his breathing without letting his gaze stray from her.

Her eyes seemed to widen, their scope of deepest black expanding furthermore, as though the deepest realms of that night were at once known to her. She dropped into a bow, slow and deliberate, her neck rounding as her front end sunk to the river's surface. The white shape of her dropped into the water yet did not rise or writhe as he expected. The water surface became still for a few seconds, before the rise of something small and white broke its peace once again. A small, perfectly formed lily flower breached the surface and settled quite still upon the spot that Sanna had disappeared.

He watched it, mesmerised and no more calm. His heavy breath punctured the still night, as everything around him seemed in a lull. The lily was an assault on all his preconceptions about life and reality. He found his way home in the dark. His mind as troubled on his return as when he'd left.

Hugh had no intention of answering the door, but on the third round of knocking he found the strength to get up from his seat. Dylan buzzed around his legs like an excitable dog. He opened the front door and saw Liana, her skin pale and her hair listless.

"Can we talk?" she said. Dylan bobbed on the spot, unable to stay still.

"Stay here Dylan," Hugh said flatly.

Dylan's face crumbled, but he didn't protest as he watched Hugh slip his trainers on and step outside, closing the door behind him. He went to the window to watch as they entered the long grass of the garden, Liana leading, Hugh hanging back with dragging feet. Movement caught his eye, and his eyes widened as he glimpsed a figure in a dark jacket moving behind the outhouse. His small hands gripped the windowsill, but he stayed watch.

"Are you ok?" Liana asked.

"I've barely slept."

"Oh, Hugh-" she began, breaking off as she leaned into him. "I can't believe what's happened. And we were there, we saw all it all."

He felt her breathing against his chest, her hair brushing against his neck as she sought comfort from him. He was like a rock, hardened from the inside and detached from all emotion. He let one hand come to rest against her shoulder, but his body wouldn't relax. She pulled away.

"What are we going to do?" she asked.

"There's no need for you to be involved anymore. Just forget about it all."

"But I want to help. I can't just leave you alone with this."

He looked straight at her for the first time, trying to be more assertive than he felt.

"No. I should never have told you."

"Don't do this to me Hugh, don't push me away." She touched his arm again, the muscle taught. "Do you even know who this man is? Or what he is? You call him a friend, but if that's true then why is he doing this to you?"

"I can handle it."

"Can you?" She lowered her voice. "Can you handle Kain as well?"

"What's Kain got to do with anything?"

"You should be careful. I got the feeling he meant what he said the other night. I don't think he'll let it go."

"I'm not scared of Kain." He laughed; a fleeting, strangled sound that did little to elicit a smile from Liana. She looked at him with a pained sympathy he could hardly bear.

"Look, there's nothing to be worried about. They're not even here anymore, they left the next day."

"Really? Just like that?"

"Yeah. They won't be coming back. Even if they did, I could handle it, I can handle Kain and all of it. I'm fine." He tried to smile, tried to relax a little.

"You don't look fine," she said. "I wish you'd be honest with me."

The words slipped out before she could stop herself. She analysed his face, waiting for an explosion or some rebuttal, but he was silent. Hugh was looking past her now, studying the house, savouring the feel of the wind against the rough skin of his face.

"I'm here for you," she said, her voice fading away. "If you want me."

She came close to him again and this time he let her sink into his arms and mould her body against his. He held her until she pulled away. There was nothing more to say.

Kain watched Liana disappear down the long driveway, fighting the impulsive urge to intercept her and make her spill her secrets. The house loomed quiet and dark, its windows shielded with drawn curtains. That suited him, for he had picked up on their gestures and Liana's nervous glances. He would find out their secrets now, by whatever means required.

He stuck to the edge of the wild garden, keeping a furtive eye on the house. When he reached the trees, the woods leered over him like an impenetrable barrier, their coarse blockade seemed to claim dominion over further ground. But he traced the treeline until he found a path, the ground dry with footfall.

His sense of anticipation grew as he followed the path. There was little in the way of searching, merely his anxious curiosity that led him to the clearing. Many hours of turning over incessant questions in his mind seemed to finally be relinquished as he found what he searched for. A small clearing, dappled light from above. The river burbled like a water feature at one end. But in the foreground, he looked down at what it was he now knew he'd been looking for; a crude log seat and a pile of whitened ash. On the ground, a porcelain bowl with the crusted remains of heated oats.

Chapter 14

Hugh woke in the evening, feeling somewhat rested and far better than he had earlier in the day. Even his throat had improved, although a tentative feel of his neck told him that the underside of his jaw was still swollen and tender. He had to empty his bladder, and on the way to the bathroom saw that Dylan had found his bed. He was sprawled out snoring on top of the covers. The opportunity for a quiet evening opened up before him.

The lights were on downstairs, but his mother wasn't in the living room when he poked his head round the door to check her usual resting spot. The coffee table had been cleared of clutter, a full plastic carrier bag on the floor next to it. Puzzled, he went to the kitchen to make a hot drink. When he pushed open the door and saw the scene that awaited him, all plans for his evening were blotted in an instant.

His mother lay curled on the dirty linoleum with her head against the wooden sideboard. Next to her, a puddle of vomit, like that which also covered the sink, was putrid and staling. There was a tipped glass on the counter, its water contents pooling around a mess of pens and fridge magnets. She was making awful, guttural groaning noises; Her hair clung with sweat to the sallow skin of her face, and her hands clasped at her stomach with fingers like claws that wished for no skin.

He rushed forward and dropped to her side, taking her hands and trying to pull her from the floor.

"Mum, Mum! What's happened?" Panic morphed his voice into an octave closer to Dylan's than his own. His mother only grimaced; every part of her face contorted with pain.

"Sit up mum, please," he pleaded, applying force to her arms, her back, but with no release. She would not move. His foot slipped into the vomit in his distraction. He half stood, not wanting to release hold of his mother, but he needed to find the house phone. It wasn't in the receiver or on the countertop, but by the sink he noticed his mother's depression medication, decanted, the lid at its side.

At his feet, his mother bent at her middle, succumbing to incomprehensible mutterings. He grabbed a cloth from the sink and wetted it with cold water. Dabbing it against her skin, he tried to get her to focus on him.

"Did you take the pills mum? How many did you take?" She shook her head, although whether to his question or the misery of her situation he didn't know. "I have to ring the ambulance, you need a doctor." he said, beginning to cry. To his horror, he saw his mother's own tears breaking free from between her closed eyelids. She grabbed at him, holding him with a grip like death.

"No, Hugh. No ambulance," she said, the effort of speaking beaded a new crop of sweat on her face.

"Mum, I have to."

She opened her eyes wide, with a clarity that shocked him.

"No. Help me to bed. I'll be ok."

She didn't look ok. The smell of vomit pervaded the kitchen. He was caught between staying with her or rushing to get his phone. He dithered in a frantic moment of indecision until she started to grope at the sideboard and try to stand. On instinct, he helped her. They made slow progress out of the kitchen and towards her bedroom. Vomit stuck to her clothing and her hands were wet against his side; whether with water, sick or sweat he did not know. The stairs were the most difficult; his mother's feet dragged up and over every step. Halfway up, an attack of nausea sent her crashing to the floor as if a convulsion had struck her middle. He thought of his brother. Please God don't let Dylan witness this.

Once they reached the top, shakes took hold of her entire body, but it was a short way to the bed now. He pulled the cover over her. Her breathing was shallow and laboured from the pain and exertion of it all, but he stayed by her side and listened to it settle. After a few minutes, she nestled into the covers as though cold, and though her tucked arms and knees gave away her pain, her face began to relax.

"Why did you do it, Mum?" he asked. His mother didn't open her eyes; she would look almost peaceful if it wasn't for her pallid colour and the grubby tear tracks that cut through the sweat and the grime.

"You deserve better than me," she said. "You're better off me being gone."

"Why would you say that?"

"He was right. He told me. Keep the doors locked." Her face twisted with pain and cut off her voice as she tensed to let it pass.

Hugh's breathing had stilled at her words. He looked at her, horrified.

"Don't call the hospital, please."

He turned away, unable to look at her whilst she suffered like this. Her words repeated through his mind, remembering her strange behaviour since the night Gamel had first come, whenever darkness fell.

He found his phone and called the nearest relatives he knew. He had to speak to somebody. The wait for them to arrive was torturous. He hovered on the landing, checking on his mother, his brother, and the window in turn.

On their arrival, he let his aunt and uncle in and led them to the bedroom. He hung back by the doorway, afraid her eyes would seek out his own and condemn him for not leaving her to die. They bustled all around her, a mix of voices coming together in panic and questions.

He couldn't listen to it.

He was right. He told me. She had said. But told her what? *You deserve better than me. You're better off me being dead.*

Had Gamel really said something like that? In his heart he knew.

Keep the doors locked. He would do one better he thought, you need not lock the doors if nobody's trying to get in. A single thought emerged from the chaos of his mind. It centered on Gamel, and was coloured with hot rage for his mother, for her suffering.

He slipped on his boots.

Unaffected by total blackness of the night and the howl of the wind that wound through the trees in great gusts like agonised banshees, he went to the clearing with a determined single mindedness. He had no fear. The woodland which so often appeared graver, more animated in the nighttime now seemed to shrink back from him, as if it sensed his indifference to its dark corners tonight. The clearing was unoccupied, but the glowing embers of a snubbed fire still smoked in a heap near the trees.

"Show yourself! I need to speak to you now."

He tried to sound collected, in control, but it was a poor effort. He sounded just as he felt and he knew Gamel would be wise to it. There was nothing but silence. He picked up a nearby branch with ferocious speed despite its weight. Swinging his whole body, he flung it onto the fire wishing to quash the embers that burned there, sending a flurry of ashes into the air.

"Come and speak to me!" he roared, losing his composure. He kicked the remnants of the fire in his frustration, not caring for the state of his boots that struck the wood and charred remains. The thought of his mother came rushing to the forefront of his mind. He succumbed to heavy sobs, his body and mind broken down.

"Why did you do it? You said you would help, not make everything worse. I don't want her to die," he said to the empty wilds. He dropped to the floor in a squat position, holding his head.

"You never should have pulled me out the water. I wish you hadn't. My mum wouldn't have done what she has. You would have left her alone."

His body was shaky and weak, but his voice was a renewed pit of fire, replaced by a new, far fiercer pain. He picked up a smoldering stick that lay in the skeletal fire at his feet, using it to strike the nearest tree with all his force, ignoring the shock of the impact that rattled his arm and the rip of violent friction against the soft skin of his palm. He hauled it towards the water shotput style, sending it high into the air before it descended with a great splash that was sure to spook all nearby living creatures.

"I never want to see you again."

He left that place a dead ground, certain that he left no one in the shadows. As he came out from the trees, he saw the pulsing blue lights of an ambulance.

They had found a safe refuge in Dylan's room as the only place that felt safe and calm. Behind Hugh's head, his brother's empty hand twitched beneath the blow of soft exhalations that emerged from the small o of his mouth and died just before they reached Hugh's ear.

It had taken a long time for him to settle Dylan, who had been screaming and resisting the restraint of their uncle when he'd returned. They watched their mother being wheeled into the bright, sterile bowels of the ambulance. He had taken Dylan and pressed his face to his chest, blotting his tears on the fabric of his shirt.

Once in his bedroom, he'd nestled Dylan in the crook of his arm and soothed him with gentle murmurs until his mouth dried and his lips cracked. The little catches in Dylan's breath subsided and his body grew heavy and limp. Here he remained in a small sanctuary of quiet, his legs and neck stiffening as he tried to stave off sleep.

His aunt was asleep in the sitting room. She had cleared a space on the sofa and curled there with a thin sheet, wanting comfort more than warmth. The mahogany wall clock said that it was half-past two in the early hours. But not all was still or asleep in the farmhouse this hour. Outside the kitchen window, large hooves flattened the dewy grass and met with a spattering of loose pavestones with a dull clop sound. Sanna breathed deeply and her exhalation hit the window glass in a spread of short-lived condensation. One of Gamel's four fingered hands settled on the breadth of her neck. He let out a desolate sigh that transcended the wake of two hundred years or more.

It was difficult to see much through the opaque glass that faced them. The light inside was off and the outside pane had not seen a cleaner for a very long time. Old grime and moss had made its home on what had once been a varnished wooden frame. A dim reflection of them both, an old man and his horse which looked to lack eyes, and rather gaze emptily with two gaping holes that saw nothing, stood in the way of much a view inside.

That heavy sigh which reminded him of the past also put him in touch with his basic instinct, which was to turn and walk away from the lights and presence of strange people. This was not his home or his land. His feet moved in sympathy with his thoughts and he turned to face the woods that beckoned him. They slid against gravel and the sudden scrape of stone awakened even more so that basic fear of bringing attention to himself that had kept him safe and alive for so long, even after others of his kind.

But there was an inexplicable pull that prevented him from leaving the house untouched. He couldn't be sated with a mere glance at its innards before tracing away like a spirit that walked the earth in patched leather boots, pulled apart at the seams. He was drawn to Hugh and wished only to see that he was safe. In the clearing, Gamel had left before hearing him finish. The message had been clear, the damage had been done, and the injury to the boy was immense. He resolved that he would not imprint on his life again, for to do so could bring nothing good.

Yet here he was. He would check on the boy. Put his mind at ease before leaving Hugh to the bidding of times slow censure on his memory of the past few weeks. He summoned once again the movement of his reluctant, weary feet and approached the back door with caution. He reached into one of many deep pockets and pulled out a brass key. Sanna stood relaxed on the paving with her ears drooping sleepily to the side, one back hoof propped up on the toe as she rested.

The pungent smell of the kitchen struck him. The acrid quality of vomit was the most pervasive, but it mingled with the chemical odour of cleaning solution. These were the two strongest smells, but there were more to concern him. It was faint, at first only a trace, but he identified the foreign odour of perfume. It was the smell of a new person, that came from a different world to his own accustom. His stiff, arthritic fingers tensed, and he watched every space that confronted him with a tireless focus known only by those with an acute sense of imminent danger.

He passed through the kitchen and the hallway leading to the stairs. He left the door to the sitting room untouched, sensing the smell and sound of a stranger within. After creeping up the stairs with a lightness of foot he didn't naturally possess, he found both Hugh's and his mother's room empty, his heart clamping cold with fear and grim foreboding. But he remembered the small brother of Hugh, the young child who'd glimpsed him briefly. He went to the last remaining room and pressed against the door. It creaked at the hinge, but the two boys inside hardly stirred. Hugh was curled on the floor, his arms forming a crutch for his head and his body huddled as if he felt the cold in absence of a sheet. Gamel stood for far longer than he would usually dare under the influence of sense, but he wanted to be sure that the boy was safe. He wanted to figure it out. His heart seemed to beat even more fervently than before. He realised that he cared for Hugh a great deal more than he should.

There was a fleecy blanket at the foot of the bed. Gamel stepped forward, but the floorboard creaked under his weight. He cursed the burden of such heavy, boot clad feet, watching for any movement from the boys as he came close. He took the blanket in his hand, its soft fleece catching on the rough skin of his fingers. Hugh was within touching distance.

He started to stir, a twitch of the hand, a squint of his eyes, but then his legs kicked out and he rolled onto his back. Gamel froze. He cast Hugh into a deep sleep. Bending stiffly at his middle, he dropped the blanked over Hugh's legs. He reached into his pocket and took out the once shiny tourism leaflet that had been with him for so long. White worn creases marked its areas of folding and where the elements had reached its now lackluster sheen. There was little space amongst the pictures and the information covering each side, but just enough for what he needed.

He left the door slightly open, padding downstairs in the dark. In the hallway he paused, considering what he'd done.

The sound of flowerpots falling and crashing against stone reached him from outside. There was no time. He left the house and found Sanna standing by the sitting-room window, nuzzling the glass. Broken flower pots and an overturned tin bucket lay by her hooves. She acknowledged him with a lazy swish of her tail.

"Come Sanna," he said, his words tumbling out on one tired breath.

They returned to the woodland in silence.

Chapter 15

Hugh sat up, his whole body aching. He kicked Dylan's blanket off his legs, where it had become tangled in the night. Something dropped to the floor. Bleary-eyed, he found a pencil stub by his feet next to an old leaflet that looked ready for the bin. He unfolded it, taking care not to rip it where the creases were so deep. There was a small logo for Visit England above a photo of a perfect blue lake, bordered with lush green hills and bountiful trees. The colours had faded and a network of creases spread across it like veins, forgotten in a pocket for years.

He opened it, scanning over more words and photos, all selling the prospect of visiting and staying in England. On the back, a white background displayed small boxes with further details. Distinctive, messy scrawl cut across them in a slant: "*I was trying to help.*"

He read it slowly, studying each word as if it were not English. With a heavy feeling in his chest he slipped the leaflet into the pocket of the jeans he'd slept in. It felt as if it may fracture into pieces at the slightest stress.

In the kitchen, both boys sat down to eat breakfast whilst their aunt was cleaning. Dylan was subdued and pale. Hugh found the milk sickly and the cereal unpalatable, sticking with every swallow.

"I spoke to the hospital this morning," his aunt said from the sink. "They said she's had a good night's rest after the stomach pump and they'll have more of an update on when she can come home after the consultant's been round to see her this morning."

Hugh looked down at his bowl, trying to push away the image of his mother all alone in a strange hospital ward.

"I think-" his aunt started. She was peering out of the window, her nose almost touching the glass. "I think there's someone in the garden."

He pushed his chair back from the table and went to the window.

"Where?"

"They went into those trees."

The leaves shimmied in a Mexican wave at his approach, with a gust that seemed to stir through him in the same way, as if he too possessed the same frailty as the hanging shreds of green. The clouds swarmed and turned to putrid grey overhead. His feet settled on the dirt without a sound as he tried to see through the trees, looking for Gamel.

At the place where the small side path split off from the main track and curved towards the clearing, an explosion of sound made him jump as a fat pheasant burst from the shrubbery and flew away in a screeching mass of feathers. He recovered his breath, but made no further move for ahead of him a figure came out from the trees. It was Kain. His gait was stilted and his face cast in shadow.

"Carry on," Kain said.

"What are you doing here?"

"Carry on where you were going, although I already know. You're going to that place by the river where your friend camps out."

"Let it go Kain. You're wasting your time." Hugh tried to turn away but Kain moved forwards to meet him, commanding his attention.

"Do you think I'm joking? I'm serious when I say, I will know what you're hiding."

"I've got nothing to hide."

"Who is he then?" Kain closed the distance between them, looking Hugh directly in the eyes. "Tell me what you know."

Hugh looked away, his mouth turning up in a smirk. Kain shoved him on one shoulder.

"Look at me," Kain demanded. "Don't make me hurt you."

"They're gone. I told you you're wasting your time."

"What did you say to Liana then? I saw you two talking." Hugh looked at the ground, wishing he could escape. He could feel his face flushing red.

"Tell me!" Kain shouted. Hugh met his gaze.

"No."

"Then you're lying. You won't tell me because they're still here."

"No. I won't tell you because I don't trust you."

Kain dropped his head and made a sound like brief laughter. When he looked back up at Hugh, his eyes were red and bright.

"So I'm still not good enough for you."

A blow from one of Kain's fist struck him on the left cheek, knocking the air from him. His hands rushed to his swelling face.

"They're gone. They're not here anymore," he insisted, but another hit spun the world out of view in a blur of green and brown and red. The floor greeted him with a lurching thud, his hands and face grazing the stones. His vision began to focus again. He drew his shaking arms away from his head where he had curled and settled against the dirt that was so cool against the fire of his face. He saw the bright red of Kain's trainers walking away.

Back at the house he went straight to the bathroom. He kept his trainers on and his head down in a bid to go unnoticed. He made it to the top of the stairs before a bump and a patter of feet came from Dylan's bedroom. He put out a hand as he slipped into the bathroom and locked the door.

"Wait Dylan, not now."

He tuned out the simpering sound of Dylan's complaints and turned to the sink. A small mirror stood on the windowsill above it, set back amongst disuses toiletry bottles and grimy soap bars. He pulled it forward and wiped away some of the dust with his hand. He studied a face that was unfamiliar to him. One eye was grossly distorted, a lump of swelling and fresh bruising beneath his eyebrow. On the other side, his cheek had flowered in a dark spread of discolour, the imprint of a fist. He wetted some toilet roll and pressed it to his eye.

"Hugh? Hugh, I need you," Dylan whined from the other side of the door.

"Hold on," he shouted, turning back to his face in the mirror. There was no way of hiding it. He splashed his face with cold water and dried himself with a stagnant towel. Dylan was still waiting for him.

"What happened?" Dylan asked, worry lines crossing his forehead. "Your face is hurt."

"I just had an accident, it's nothing."

Dylan didn't question his brother as he followed him downstairs to the kitchen, all the time shooting anxious glances at his face. Hugh made them both lunch before passing the afternoon with Dylan, losing himself in their make believe world where vague evil plans could be scuppered by stick guns and super powers of mere noise.

At the dinner table, Hugh couldn't hide his face well enough to avoid his aunt's notice.

"What happened?" she asked.

"He had an accident," Dylan said. Hugh concentrated on his food.

"Well, I have news from the hospital." Both boys stopped eating and looked at her. "Your mum's coming home, after just a bit more monitoring. She'll be having some home visits from the doctor but importantly, she's ok."

Dylan squealed with excitement and Hugh's stomach unclenched. Dylan grabbed his arm, wanting to share his joy.

"There has been some discussion though, about what's best going forward. Dylan, you're going to come on a little holiday to our house to let your mum recover and have a break."

"What? He doesn't need to go anywhere," Hugh said.

"It's just for a week or two. We'll go out on trips and have some treats too, it'll be fun."

"He's not used to being away. I can look after him fine," he insisted, but his aunt put up her hand.

"Your mother's agreed to it. It's what's best."

The living room was unrecognisable since being tidied, so after dinner they went to Hugh's room to watch a film. Hugh held Dylan close to him whilst he tried to stay awake. When the end credits rolled, he got Dylan changed and tucked him into his own bed, squeezing in next to him and listening to him drift into sleep. There was nothing on his phone to entertain him, so while dusk became darkness outside, he reached for a book. It was a well-thumbed copy of Alice in Wonderland, once borrowed from a library but never returned. He read of falling down a rabbit hole and unexplainable happenings, eventually finding his own fretful sleep.

The next day came upon Hugh as a burgeoning cold, unpleasant and unstoppable. A sadness came upon him he had once thought lifted. In many ways, Dylan had been his sole company for most of the years they'd spent in the large, breezy house of many corners and the wild grounds it rested in. The prospect of silence and solitude with no escape terrified him.

He trailed behind as Dylan ran through the long grass to the edge of the woodland. It was the closest he'd been since he'd last seen Sanna.

"Can we play in the woods?" Dylan asked. "You can choose what we play."

"Not today. Let's stay in the garden."

Dylan pulled a face.

"But the woods is better for dens."

Hugh considered it for a moment, but a heavy cover of cloud had blocked the sun like a rolling juggernaut and the trees seemed to stand before them like a black well of depthless danger.

"Not today."

"Is it because of that man? Is he not your friend anymore?" Dylan's eyes traced over the fresh bruising on his brother's face.

"Don't worry about him anymore. Come on."

Dylan followed him to the play frame, where they spent the rest of a humid August afternoon.

When they returned to the house, the atmosphere was busy and tense. Dylan's things were packed and ready. At the sound of a car, both boys went to the door. Their uncle approached the house, dragging their mother's bags at his side. Behind him, their mother emerged. She looked exhausted and in desperate need of a dark room in which to lie. Her smile on seeing them lit up the rest of her dull features. Both boys greeted her with a hug, Dylan's gripping and lingering, Hugh's brief and awkward.

Their mother made it to one of the kitchen chairs with what seemed like the last of her energy. Hugh stayed quiet, knowing that he and his mother would have plenty of time to talk if needed, and it was Dylan who was desperate for her attention.

"I don't want to go," he said with wet eyes, pulling softly at her hands.

"It's only for a short while sweetie, and then when you come back, I'll be feeling well enough so we can have lots of fun together."

"Please feel better quickly, Mummy."

"I'll do my best."

This seemed to satisfy Dylan, and they shared a gentle moment before their aunt and uncle came through the door and said that they ought to be leaving.

"Wait!" Dylan cried and threw his arms around his mother, pressing himself against her chest, where he could smell her dried sweat. When he spoke, his voice was muffled but still clear. "Make sure Hugh doesn't go near the woods. There's a bad man in there."

"What? What bad man?" she said. She looked at Hugh but he wouldn't meet her gaze. Dylan was clasping his middle tightly as he said goodbye. He had to work hard not to let his emotion overcome him as he hugged him back.

A few minutes later, the sound of the car faded away leaving the house to lapse into silence. His mother slumped as soon as they had gone. With only Hugh for company, she didn't need to put on a brave face.

They both spent the evening alone. When midnight passed and Hugh's thoughts turned to sleep, he went downstairs to check the locks. His mother was in the kitchen, settled in the old upholstery chair with a cup of cold tea by her side. She was watching the night through the window. Hugh said nothing as he passed through the room and checked the back door was shut and bolted. On his return, his mother broke the silence.

"You didn't need to check the lock. I'd already done it twice."

The rough quality of her voice startled Hugh, and he turned to check if she'd been drinking. It didn't look like it, but that was usually the case when she was raspy and her words merged at each end.

"I just wanted to be sure," he said between mouthfuls of tap water.

"Dylan mentioned something." She paused to check he was listening. "Something about a man in the woods." Hugh put his glass by the sink.

"He's got a good imagination."

His mother resumed her watching through the window and cradled her cup of tea.

"Was it the man that hit you?"

"No. It was someone else."

His mother continued to sit and stare, her lips sealed and her eyes distant.

Hugh lingered, contemplating that which was unsaid.

"I'm glad you're back mum."

She pursed her lips, the thin slit of her eyes moistening.

He headed for the door, but she stopped him halfway.

"Hugh? When did we start keeping so many secrets from each other?"

He stood in the doorway's shadow, thinking of what he could share and yet instantly discarding it, for years of a difficult relationship and little communication could not be erased in a matter of days.

"Are we safe?" she asked.

"He's not coming back."

By the time his mother left the kitchen, the sky had begun to brighten and her bed had grown cold.

The house was unbearably quiet, an empty shell. Without Dylan to brighten it, he couldn't help but see it for the dingy, cluttered space it really was. His mother's sparse company only served as a constant reminder of her illness. The harmonious marriage between apathy and inactivity resulted in an atmosphere so stale, so depressive; he could no longer bear it. He grabbed his jacket and stepped out into the rain, not bothering to raise his hood. The trees soon sheltered him.

He sat on the ground after a few minutes, not caring for his jeans on the damp earth. Recent rainfall had swelled the river. He watched it flowing a more forceful pass between its banks as in the back of his mind he thought of the person he hoped to see, but did not dare to seek. He had never felt so alone.

He bought out a pen and a slip of paper from his jacket pocket, chewing its end whilst he thought. Decided, he wrote a few words in his usual slanted style and placed it folded by Gamel's log, weighting it down with a rock. The message was simple; it expressed his purest wish.

"Please come back."

Chapter 16

It was all coming together now, Hugh's recurring visits to the woods, fragments of information like pieces of a puzzle. She was fairly certain that his own interest in den building and playing wild Indians had waned by the age of twelve, and it was only by Dylan's persistence that he'd been to the woods since. But that wasn't quite true, not in recent weeks.

The unknown burned inside her. Fine company to unanswered questions was the fear that never left. The thought of how her son might be linked to her own haunting terrified her. So did the prospect of what lurked amongst the trees.

She had her own ghosts haunting her thoughts. She knew how a house should be, a family, and it was not like this. Her after dinner pill caught in her throat. Going into the woods alone tonight was a reckless idea, but she regarded the prospect with less apprehension than the thought of confronting Hugh upstairs.

Her own back garden was as new to her. It was like an exotic land, full of new sounds, sensations and smells. It had been so long since she'd stepped into this wild grass that had sprung up with such fervent speed that she marveled at what had always been here. As familiar as it was alien, her feet found the path to the trees. Her soft, dolly shoes darkened with the dirt, and she could feel every undulation and hard rock or root as she walked on through the dark. When the path ended, she pushed on, thinking of Hugh. Clawing branches snagged at her arms and legs and crawling things scattered at her step.

The river was up ahead. The ground sloped away to meet the water where it spread out like a great heinous gulf to part the trees. She stopped on the bank. High above, in the small scrape of visible sky, the clouds joined in a grey gathering, whipping up the evening air and darkening all below. It was a lonely land, where life was a secret thing and to speak and exist were to strike a clashing chord with nature's barren peace. If only Hugh would speak to her.

A dash of colour caught her eye. An object of delicate white and pink that broke the block of dirty grey water. It was a solitary flower floating upstream. She got closer, stretching to see. Its splayed petals stretched above the water's surface. Soft like velvet, free floating against the current. Her right foot crept forwards with the tilt of her weight. Water seeped onto the canvas of her shoe.

There was a sound, a cry; animal or human she couldn't discern. She looked behind her, waiting for something or someone to make themselves known. But there was only silence. She turned back to the river and jumped at the sight of a white horse, stood in the river's midst where it was deepest, the water grazing its belly. Was it real? God knows she was used to questioning her sense of reality. But there were dark flecks of detail on its muzzle, the quiet lowing of its breath. The horse's coat was a dull white, clinging to its sharp wither and protruding hips. It must be sick. A memory came to her of one of those nature documentaries she'd once watched, in which it had said that many animals will seek solitude before death. Was it dying? As if on cue, the horse seemed to sway slightly, as though weak legs struggled to hold its weight.

Janet reached out a pale hand, beckoning to the lonely animal. It looked up and seemed to really see her for the first time, see inside her. It moved towards her, coming out of the water and up the bank with steady steps. Janet's breath hitched in her throat as she moved to meet it, placing her outstretched hand on the horse's head, caressing it around the eyes and forelock. It felt deathly cold, streaked grey with the river.

"There, there," she said, finding her voice. "Aren't you

beautiful?" The horse reached its head into the nook of her body, its eyes closing in a gesture of trust. "Oh," Janet said, surprised by the horse's desire to be close. "You're so cold."

The horse pushed its head into her, making her step back. It came to her side, curling its neck and pushing her again so she was forced to step again towards the bank.

"Stop," Janet said, putting her hand out. Rather than the placid animal of a moment ago, the horse's ears flicked back. In an instant, its nose was above her head, its body turning to block her exit. There was a second of panic, before seeing only white as the horse hit her like a solid wall. It sent her plunging backwards down the bank, losing her footing as she plummeted into the icy river. The cold murkiness enveloped her in an instant. This was not the smooth free-fall of someone meeting the resistance of the water like a kiss, this was the thrashing panic of the primal urge to stay in touch with the oxygen all at once robbed from you. The close of death wrapped around her, a great weight holding her down while her eyes were blinded with dirty, stinging water and the frantic kicking of legs.

She both feared and fought to find the bottom of the river, trying to push up towards the surface and dry ground. Her pursed mouth broke out into open air that she gulped into her throat, dry with fear. The horse was behind her. She had no time to look, the entire world coming into focus in an explosion of sight and sound before a blow like a pair of mallets manned with heavy hands struck her back.

This time she had no intake of breath to buy time. She pushed and fought, looking for the breach between mute black and starry sky. But what had surrounded her before now found its way inside. Bright blooms of pain began to burst inside her as the river water scorched her airway and made her part of the inhospitable realm she was fighting to break free from.

With one last effort she found its edge, breaking through it like a hatchling that with its dying breath burst upon freedom. Her ears came clear of the water and heard a shout.

"Nykur!" There was a flurry of movement and the roar of displaced water as the horse ran from her side. She tried to look for whoever had spoken, a faceless voice that she'd heard before, but slipped into an unwilling sleep. This time she fell, it was with that soft grace that might be dreamt of.

Chapter 17

Hugh pushed away his laptop and sat up in his bed. Only the steady tick of his clock occupied the room. He felt the periphery want for food and stimulation, but more than anything else he could no longer stand the quiet of the house. He acknowledged the sour pit of his stomach and the longing for Dylan's happy company, but when he went downstairs, it was not to resolve either of those issues. He was looking for his mum.

He found the light switch and brightened the cold corridor. Clutter mounds and dark corners lit up before him, but there was still no sound or movement other than his own. Both the living room and the kitchen were empty. The stairs were a blur beneath his feet as he ran back up them. He retrieved his phone from where it had been charging by his bed, dialling her number with trembling fingers before pressing its cool surface to his hot ear. It rang out.

Where was she? She wasn't in the house, and he couldn't stand around idle. He tried her phone again downstairs. There was an answer this time, the sound of her ring tone, the default buzz, coming from the kitchen table beneath today's letter pile. There was no note, no explanation. She never went out, hadn't socialised in years. There was no one he wanted to call. No other explanation than the worst.

Three loud raps sounded at the back door. He ducked down and dodged away from the uncovered window, his whole body on high alert. The knocking came again, more insistent this time. He'd have to answer it. His heart was trying to jump ship and his skin felt electric. He shuffled to the counter half crouched, reaching for the knife block and pulling one out. Now he could approach the door.

With a single push, the door swung open and illuminated a small arc of the back step. Gamel was just beyond its reach, leaning one arm against the wall with a grim expression. His heavy-lidded eyes appraised Hugh with a mixture of relief and alarm. Hugh moved the knife behind his back, but not before Gamel noticed.

"Put that bleedin' thing down. Your mor's in the woods."

"Is she ok?"

"She should be, but I need you to get her home. Come with me."

Hugh put the knife down and ran to Gamel's side as he walked stiffly towards the trees. Despite his worries for his mum, he felt happiness wash over him. Gamel was back, and he still cared.

"She's had a brush with Sanna," Gamel said over his shoulder. "I got her out of there before any real harm was done."

"But you left her, she's out there all alone?"

"She's sleeping, perfectly safe. I haven't the strength or the will to move her more than I already have."

They passed beneath the branches; the woodland appearing as a great tumour on the landscape, blotting stars and moonlight with its thick canopy. Gamel's pace did not slow.

"I'm glad to see you," Hugh said, unable to come up with anything better to describe the way he felt. "Did you get my note?"

"I'm glad to see you too, after the other night."

"I'm sorry for what I said."

"There's no need to be. You had every right to be upset, and I'm very sorry for any part I played in what happened. I wouldn't ever want to hurt you like that." He paused, his heavy breathing punctuated with soft footfall. "I was trying to help in my cack-handed way, if you can believe that. I wanted her to understand. I probably should have learned my lesson the first time I got involved."

They walked in thoughtful silence for a minute. Hugh didn't want this moment to slip away, leaving things unsaid. It felt fragile.

"Dylan's gone," he said. "I don't know what to do anymore. It feels like I have no one left." Gamel was quiet by his side barring a soft sigh like a fractious last breath.

"Surely you must understand now that we cannot stay. It's too dangerous. With so many people involved, the longer we stay, the more likely it is that either one of us or someone else will be harmed again. It's not how we've made it this far."

"But I need you here. I don't have anyone else."

Gamel stopped and leaned against a tree trunk, catching his breath. He turned to Hugh and made sure he had his full attention.

"What do you think your mother was doing out here in the woods, by herself, in the dark? Do you think she just fancied a walk? I was never going to stay forever; you knew that from the beginning."

They came to the river bank and followed it round a long curve. As the trees thinned and Hugh could see some way ahead, a small black heap by the water came into view. He broke away from Gamel and ran to what he knew was his mother. She was covered with Gamel's frayed woolen blanket and sleeping deeply. Her skin was white and damp. He put his arms around her and wiped the hair from her face, hating the slackness of her body. She wouldn't wake, despite his shaking and calling her name. In his panic he'd forgotten that only Gamel could undo the induced repose in which she slumbered.

"Wake her up," he called over his shoulder to Gamel, who was watching a few feet away. "Undo it, she's cold."

Gamel stepped back into the dense woodland and faded out

of sight. In his arms, his mother woke. Her eyes opened and were wide with fear as she took in his face. Her hands pulled away the blanket.

"What's happened? Hugh?" He'd pulled away but was still close.

"It's ok, you're ok. We just need to get you home."

"Where are we? In the woods?" She moved to a sitting position and felt the wetness of her clothes. She looked to the water, flinching at his touch.

"Come on. You need to get warm and dry." She shuddered as if his words let in the cold. It was frightening, the way her face looked.

"Tell me," she said. "You know what happened, what's happening here. Tell me." She reached for his hand but he recoiled at the feel of her. "Please, Hugh." But he only stood, and in doing so escaped her appeal. Janet tried to stand also, but violent tremors shook her body. He helped her off the ground.

"It's this way." He was patient as he helped her, even when she wouldn't look ahead, wanting to turn and search the watching, silent trees.

Once inside, they locked the door on the harsh and inhospitable night. Thankfully, his mother was too distracted to notice the knife on the table. She looked even worse under the bright, artificial light. She'd come to a stop by the sink, her system on pause, dazed and devoid of coherent thought or direction. Hugh put on the kettle.

"You need to change out of those wet clothes into something dry," he said. With the placid willingness of a sick child, she took his instruction and went to her room. He prepared hot, sweet tea and took it to her. His mother was changed but struggling with the tangled bedding. He placed the tea on the table, pushing against the clutter to make some space.

"You need to keep warm. Drink the tea, it's hot but it'll help."

He looked at her, but his steadfast unwillingness to ever do so was brought back when she turned her face up to his with a pitiful expression.

"I don't deserve you."

"Don't say that," he snapped back, reminded of the night he'd found her on the kitchen floor.

"I meant it's supposed to be the other way round," she said. "I want to be the one taking care of you, if you'll let me."

He sniffed and turned away. At the door, he spoke over his shoulder.

"Is there anything else you want?"

"No, thank you."

With that, he left.

Chapter 18

There was still a moment of panic at the absence of Dylan in the mornings. For so long he'd been used to being woken by him, forced out of bed to attend to him and help him with breakfast. It was a hard habit to break. His mother was in a deep sleep, congealed tea half empty by her bed. He tried to shut the door to leave her undisturbed, but clutter and unwashed clothes had spread to block the doorway.

Just after midday, she met him in the kitchen.

"I was thinking," she said, collecting her thoughts. "How about we get away from here? Find a place that's smaller, where we have neighbours. It doesn't have to be far, you wouldn't need to move schools unless you want to, but I'm starting to think it might be best for us all, starting somewhere new." She looked hopefully at Hugh, who was at the table eating toast. "If you wanted-" her voice was hushed now, as if someone might overhear them. "Maybe, we could leave straight away, if it's safest. We could book a hotel, take a trip somewhere. Maybe it's just me, but I don't feel safe here anymore."

"I don't want to," he replied with the cool air of certainty. His mother looked troubled.

"I'm just so tired. I'm going to take a nap. I'll make us some dinner later."

"Whatever you say, Mum."

Evening stalked the house and his mother was still in bed. Hugh's thoughts were turning to food when his phone vibrated in his pocket. It was a message from Kain.

"I know you were lying. Your friend's going to pay tonight." It read.

He sat upright, jolted into action. There was barely a pause to pull on his trainers before sprinting to the woods, first the long grass and then the stray branches whipping at his side as he ran. Twice he tripped on hidden tree roots, so much was his haste to find the path, get to the clearing. Even with the aid of daylight it was easy to miss, and now he did, plunging blindly through indistinct darkness before realising his mistake and turning back. He was more careful now, slowing to find its narrow turn off.

He burst into the clearing, bringing his tired legs to a stop and trying to catch his breath enough to shout.

"Kain?" he called, hearing himself echo off the trees. "Gamel?"

There was movement beyond the water. "Kain?" he called again.

Gamel stepped forward from between the dark foliage, looking small amidst the high bushes, crudely dressed in his worn leather coat, his woolen cap at a tilt. His mouth was a grim line and his paling eyes were watchful and full of apprehension.

"Where's Sanna?" Hugh asked him.

"Why?"

"Where is she?"

"She often wanders by herself. She won't be too far," Gamel said.

"I need to know."

Gamel looked wary. He sank back a little into the shelter of the low leaves. "Why's that?"

Before Hugh could begin some kind of explanation, there was the sound of footfall, someone's fast approach. He turned to face the path, waiting for Kain, his mother, anyone who might be here to reproach him, but it was Liana who burst into the open space, her face flushed from running.

"Is he here? Are you ok?" She broke out into flustered questions.

"You got a message too?"

"Yeah, I came straight here. You haven't seen him?"

Hugh looked back towards the river. Gamel was gone.

"No, I haven't," he said. "Gamel? Come out, this is important." The empty space swallowed his voice. "Sanna could be in danger." He fell quiet again, studying the dark space where Gamel had stood just minutes before. Liana was restless by his side, unable to stand still, but he waited, watching. Gradually, Gamel emerged. He looked guarded, his eyes fixed on Liana. His face had lost all its usual warmth and expression. There was only what needed to be done now. What they had to do.

"Sanna is a killer, a predator," he said, his voice low. "Who could try to harm her?"

In Hugh's hand, his phone vibrated. This time there was no text, just a photo.

"I know where that is, it's near the estate," Liana said. "Hugh, we need to go."

"Were you listening?" Gamel said, a little louder now.

"It's Kain."

Chapter 19

"Hold on a minute," Kain said with a smile. The others waited while he raised his phone to take a picture. They were next to the bridge; The dim streetlights behind them only just touched the housing estate they'd walked from in the distance. They stood where the footpath changed from tarmac to dirt, where the trees closed in overhead and the wilderness began. It was a place rarely visited by him and his friends in recent years. "Let me just take this, one sec," he said. The old wooden bridge framed the right side of the photo, drawing focus to the river. It was deep here, the banks set wide apart where it coursed beneath the bridge and snaked into dense woodland.

Michael moved past him to get to the lower bank, using the length of iron pipe he'd brought to flatten and crush the long weeds. On Kain's move, the other three of their friends followed. He stooped to pick up a branch, striding through the tall grass to get to the river edge.

"How are we gonna get it to come?" Josh asked.

"Just watch," Kain said. He threw the branch into the water, its weight sending up a sizeable splash of noise and spray. It settled quickly, the night resuming its cold, still quality. The air was thick with the tension of a waiting group, but no target appeared.

"Michael, get your shoes off," Kain said. "Get in there and stir the water round a bit."

"How deep is it?"

"It's fine, we're all right here. I need to stay up here to watch out for it."

"What if it comes?"

"You've got that pipe, haven't you? That thing's going to pay for killing Ben." His face was serious, but he backed up his words with an encouraging slap on Michael's arm. Michael took off his shoes with some reluctance and left them on the ground. He had to get close to the ground to keep his balance as he lowered first one, then the other foot into the cold, fast flowing water. He reached for the bottom, trying to ignore the sucking, gritty mud that enveloped his toes as he settled his weight onto the river bed, the water up to his waist.

"It's freezing," he wheezed, drawing in great gulps of breath.

"Stir it around, use the pipe," Kain said, crouching as he fixed his view on the where the river curved away. Black water wrapped around Michael's considerable waist. He could feel the steep slope of the ground just inches from where he stood, and knew that only inches away, the water would be deep enough to carry him away.

He began moving the water, at first in wide circles against the current.

"More," Kain instructed. Michael became rougher, more exaggerated, flailing in the water like a wounded animal fighting against what held it. There was an indistinct comment from one of the others, the sound of laughter quickly shut down with a glance from Kain. He wanted silence, focus.

Perhaps it was because he was eye level with the river, but it was Michael who first saw Sanna. She was downstream, facing him. Water coursed around the length of her legs, like a breaker in the current as it hit her chest and flowed around her, making her one. Her eyes matched the darkest black, high gloss surface of the river, appearing as two parts of the continuum. Her long mane hung down her neck and between her ears, her head dropping as if exhausted, or hunting. Like the prey drive of a cat, she held an intermittent focus on Michael, fixing him with her body and her gaze, whilst her ears remained active.

"That's it lads. That's what we're here to get."

"Serious?" Lee said with a bemused expression.

"You'll see. It's a freak. Wait 'til it comes nearer."

Michael resumed his cautious stirring, watching as Sanna started to wade closer. A nervous anticipation began to build as the gathered boys took up their weapons of bats and piping. Sanna stopped a few metres away, only now appraising the group. She raised her head, nostrils wide. Indecision seemed to flash through her mind, and she looked back to where she'd come from.

"When can I get out?" Michael asked, and Sanna's attention snapped back to him. She lowered her head just enough to wet her muzzle and advanced another step.

"We'll be with you as soon as she's close enough. Come closer to the bank if you have to," Kain said. Michael looked worried, but started to edge closer to dry land. Sanna moved too. She came within an arm's length from him, his hand now firmly gripped on the smooth metal of the pipe. After a last wary glance at Kain and his friends, Sanna stretched out her nose, closing the space between her and Michael in increments until, at full extension, she could take in his smell. Michael felt the coarse brush of her whiskers on his skin.

"Kain?" he said. Kain shifted forwards, his right hand hovering by his pocket. It was a small movement, but in the water the horse's head shot upwards, her ears flattening. For a second, Michael glimpsed the white perimeter of her charcoal eyes. She could move faster than him. Her teeth rushed to take the skin of Michael's arm with vicious speed, pulling him towards the deep water with an unprecedented violence.

On the bank, Kain and the others rushed to meet the water, weapons raised. The sounds of shouting and his own cries of pain surrounded Michael as the animal greeted him again and again with gnashing teeth and kicking hooves. He struggled against the water, but the shield of his arm was bruised and bloodied, and the river began to choke him at every side. The horse was above him now like one giant, thrashing entity. It was the last thing he saw before he dropped into submersion.

They were too busy hitting and striking at every part of the animal they could reach to notice what had become of the object of its aggression. Only Kain had the presence of mind to forego joining the assault and move round to where Michael had gone under, dodging the attacking horse and the surges of water to make a grab for his friend. He got hold of some saturated material, thick with flesh beneath it, and pulled. With the horse now growing distracted by the flurry of hits on her head, neck and the top of her back, Michael pushed for air, dragging himself with the Kain's help towards shallower water.

Sanna realised that the object of her attention had escaped. She spun her hindquarters to turn on those that were beating her, lunging with her teeth and striking out with her hooves through the rain of pummeling metal as if besieged by a hail of stones. Michael started to shriek on the bank, his shouts were insistent enough that two of the boys went to help take him by the arms and pull him into the grass, where his bruised and battered body could lay limp.

Now that only Kain and Lee were left in the water, their hits grew farther between.

"What's going on?" Kain roared. Sanna turned and bit down on Lee's shoulder, leaving him screaming in pain as he scrambled for the bank. "Get back in here, all of you!" he shouted. But none of them would meet his stare.

"I'm not getting back in there," Josh said, sparking a murmur of agreement from the others.

In the river, Sanna's sides were heaving and black marks streaked her head. She turned on the spot, lashing out at the water as if disoriented. Kain watched the others help Michael to his feet and stagger back towards the houses.

"Cowards," Kain spat.

The creature was weak, and the endgame weighted his pocket.

Chapter 20

They came within sight of the bridge, and though Gamel's legs were buckling, he called out for Sanna at the sight of her. The quickest of the three, Hugh raced up the bank towards Kain. There were mere seconds to assess the scene.

At the sound of Gamel's shouts, Sanna's ears flicked back and she turned her head to look for him. Kain saw his chance. He drew the switchblade from his pocket and activated the trigger with one press. Hugh saw the flash of the knife.

"Kain! No!" He entered the river with a great splash, lunging for Kain but he was out of reach. Kain flashed him a look of wide-eyed rage and exhilaration, raising his arm to bring the knife down upon Sanna's neck. But it didn't meet its target. Kain seemed to freeze, his pale fingers clasped around the handle of the switchblade, stuck mid-course.

Sanna turned her attention back to Kain, and before Hugh could intervene, she came down on him in a sudden act of violence. She pushed him beneath her, not stopped by the resistance of her hooves against the ground as she tucked them to her belly, crashing underwater. The volume of white froth and thrashing bodies knocked Hugh back. He saw only glimpses of Sanna's white coat as she pinned her prey with teeth and body.

"No!" he cried, Liana's hysterical shouting a mere background noise. "Gamel, make her stop!" But Gamel was stock still as if transfixed. He stood in the river twenty yards away, his clothes wet through.

Driven by desperation and fear, Hugh took a length of pipe left discarded on the bank. His shouts were not enough to draw Sanna away. He got close to her, close enough to strike. He brought the metal down hard against the top of her neck, sick with the feeling of striking her. He struck again against her back, and this time it was enough to bring her head above the water's surface. They were now eye to eye, his old friend, dead or alive somewhere beneath her. Water streamed down the planes of her face and into her wild eyes. The musculature of her neck and shoulders quivered. He all at once felt the seriousness of his own vulnerability.

Hugh raised the pipe. Sanna snorted, tossing her head backwards.

"Kain? Get up," he called, but there was no response. He tried to move around her, hoping to pull Kain up from out of the water, but Sanna moved to block him. He knew it had been too long, that Kain's life was slipping away fast if it had not already conceded the fight. But he couldn't bear to leave him, now trapped by an aggressive and agitated Sanna.

"Take my hand," Liana called from the water's edge. "You need to get out, now."

He looked over, but it was an impossible distance for him to reach. Sanna made a grab at him, warding him away. He raised the pipe again, still trying to search the water's surface for any sign of Kain.

"Gamel?" he called, desperate for help. He looked down river towards where Gamel had been just moments ago, but there was only the turbid, turbulent water. Gamel had gone. His breath came hard and fast. He couldn't escape the attention of Sanna, who wished to return to where Kain had last been.

"Please," he breathed. But her neck curled and she advanced closer to him, willing to knock him down if she had to. He swung towards her with the pipe, wanting to get her away rather than connect the hit, but Sanna reacted. She took his shoulder with one lunge of her bared teeth. Shock and pain rolled through his body and he lost the pipe to the swell. He was at her mercy now. She pushed him into the water, surrendering him to the submersion of that black death. But he rolled away, just keeping his head above the surface. He sensed her coming closer. She was coming to finish him, and Liana's screams were without end.

"Nykur!" A new voice shouted, filling the open space. The water seemed to still.

"Nykur!" The call came again, clearer now. It was his mother.

He straightened, gasping for air as Sanna fled from the river. She climbed onto the opposite bank and broke into a gallop like a racehorse from the stall. The steady drumbeat of her hooves faded as she disappeared into the trees.

Hugh tried to look for his mother but his sight was blurry with dirty water and his body was a heap of pain. He felt the soft touch of a hand around his wrist, another on his back. Liana was with him, pulling him towards dry land. His mother's hand was reaching for him from the bank. He was so close, but grief and pain had exhausted his strength. The world began to fall away, a dark border closing in.

Strong arms, his mother's arms, wrapped around his upper body and pulled him skywards. It was a few minutes before he could sit up on the grass.

"He's gone, isn't he, he's dead," Liana said. Hugh didn't answer. Next to him, his mother took him in her arms. It was a kind of habit, the way Hugh had met every contact from his mother in recent years with the reproach associated with pain, shock, discomfort or all three. His mother had always recoiled likewise, not wanting to impose her touch on someone so unwilling, not wanting to push him further away. But he wanted it, needed it. He felt it in the coldness of his chest, a coldness that went down to his bones. They exchanged no words. She held him until their heartbeat came to synchronise and his breathing settled against her shoulder. His body went limp and her top became damp with fresh tears.

"It's over now," she said, looking out over the water.

"But we need to get him. We can't leave him in there," he replied. "I've got to get him out of there." He pulled away, wiping at his face like a small child.

"No," his mum said. "No one's going back in the water."

The sky was lightening as they reached home. Far behind them, blue lights reflected in the water by the bridge, as downstream, Sanna rejoined the river.

Chapter 21

There was a definite change in the air, from the lazy drag of endless sunlight to the creep of dewy mornings. The nip of autumn was close at hand. Though brief, enough time had passed for Kain's death to be old news. Hugh had made it through the hardest part, when every day had been a struggle. Now, dark moments were less frequent. It was the guilt that still hounded him.

He already felt a stranger to the trip he'd made so often throughout the summer. The clearing was empty, greeting him only with the bright chirrups of a bird high above and the soft burbling of the river. He glanced towards the log, out of habit. There was nothing out of place there, no note or item. He passed by without pause, stopping only when he was at the water's edge, his trainers finding a hold on the stony ground.

A single white rose, one he'd taken from the vase on the kitchen table, was held carefully in his hand to avoid the sharp thorns. He lowered it to the water's surface, holding it flat before he released it and watched as it sped downstream, carried by the current. When the slip of white was beyond sight and the birdsong became silence, he stood again. It was the last time he'd visit the woods. His mother had already put the farmhouse up for sale. Only the past lingered here, she'd said. She wanted to leave it far behind.

Back at the house, he put away his shoes and found his mother and Dylan in the living room. They were watching a film, but rather than the usual cartoons while their mother huddled away, lost to sleep or dark thoughts, the room was alive with the sound of bright laughter. Both of their faces were cast in a warm glow from the comedy on screen.

Hugh sat down to join them. There was nowhere else he

wanted to be.

.

Printed in Great Britain
by Amazon